SWORD

Sword of Vengeance

Alexander Karol

NEW ENGLISH LIBRARY
TIMES MIRROR

An NEL Original

*

FIRST NEL PAPERBACK EDITION DECEMBER 1973

*

NEL Books are published by
New English Library Limited from Barnard's Inn, Holborn, London, E.C.1.
Made and printed in Great Britain by Hunt Barnard Printing Ltd, Aylesbury, Bucks.

45001704 4

Chapter One

As soon as he awoke and heard the noise from the streets through his bed's curtains, Sir Harry Strang reached for his cloak, draped it over his naked shoulders, and hurried to the window to catch sight of his first view of London town by daylight. There was little for him to see. A heavy grey mist hung over the houses, which made the sharp-pointed roof-tops look sinister in the shrouds of mist. Harry wondered if the mist would remain throughout the day. By opening the casement, he could look down into the streets and the bustle of a new day in busy London reached him. The cobbles shone wetly, and across them moved porters carrying goods. There was a milk maid from the farm at Islington or Pimlico ladling milk from an urn. Soon Harry heard her 'Milk-Ho' cry as she continued up the street.

He saw a Puritan next, grim of countenance, bible cradled at his belly, hurrying along the centre of the street, hardly acknowledging the 'good morrow' of a doctor who passed him, carrying his gold-tipped stick of office. Across the way, a window clattered noisily open and Harry saw a maid tip a chamber pot's contents into the street. She held the pot far out so as not to spatter the window sill. She took no care to ensure that nobody was passing beneath the window, nor did she yell out 'Beware – the pot' as was done in county towns, and Harry was scandalised. Having finished her work and spotting Harry only a score of feet away on the opposite side of Fleet Street, she began to smirk and give him the bold eye. Harry looked away.

London, he reflected, might be a place of glitter but much of it was tarnished. If standards were often higher than in the provinces, they were often lower too. It had struck him forcibly on his arrival the night before. The noise, the smells, the eternal bustle called for a strong stomach and a clear head, for how could so many vehicles, animals and human beings rush so madly through the narrow, winding and unlit streets without there being mighty collisions?

And there had been other dangers. The innkeeper at the village of Knightsbridge had advised him not to venture into the city alone now that night had fallen, even though he had a stout right arm, a sword and saddle pistols, and a strawberry mare which had been born for speed.

Footpads lurked in the fields and woods on the Hyde Park and Belgravia side of the road he was told, and it was best to wait until a convoy of travellers had gathered so that they could enter together. Strang had been impatient, anxious to be gone and into the exciting city he had waited so long to see. He had been suspicious of the landlord, wondering if he exaggerated to keep patrons drinking his fine but expensive North Brown Ale. But when they had left, a dozen horsemen all together, with a link-boy running ahead with a blazing torch, Strang had seen the rotting corpses of several footpads hanging on gibbets by Hyde Park Gate.

It was a reminder for him that he was in a violent, seething, angry, ambitious, and rushing metropolis. All the political and religious hates of a nation met and exploded in London, and here clever and ambitious men crossed word and sword. His maternal grandmother – who was also grandmother to the Earl of Rochester – had given him solemn warning. 'Go not to that hateful place.' But Rochester was here and surviving and where but to London should a young man go who had blood in his veins and ideas throbbing in his brain?

He knew he would find much there to horrify him, but he would be ready for it. Nevertheless he ran into trouble almost immediately, before he had been in the city longer than fifteen minutes.

When he reached the Strand, which was better illuminated than other streets by the lights from the houses, the party had separated, and Strang had been directed to his accommodation in Fleet Street. In the Strand, which was slightly wider than the other streets through which he had passed, he stopped his horse a moment to survey the scene. The smells were ripe, assailing his nostrils, but the excitement was still toxic. He looked at the more sumptious houses around him, his horse drawn to one side of the street to allow the heavy traffic by. The heavy coaches, usually drawn by four or six horses, made a fearful racket as the hard iron wheels rattled over the round cobbles. Cries of 'Clear the way' rent the air as link-boys charged on ahead of their employers.

Strang sat on his horse awhile, looking at the tall houses which tilted together from the top, where the rooms were larger, and which looked like silent lovers trying to meet their neighbours across the street.

Like any newcomer to an exciting place, he looked on any stranger he met with a ready smile. All men could be his friend, for he had not been here long enough to have an enemy. But an enemy there was, even though these were his first minutes in London. The man, a gentleman by his sumptuous habit, came fast from a side lane, mounted on a spirited horse, and determined to keep close to the houses beneath the overhang (a choice place) clearing everybody in his way.

Strang heard the harsh clip of horse's hooves. The horse, a grey, came charging round the corner, the rider low, his cloak billowing. The charger was about to hit his mount, head to side, at about the point where Strang was mounted, and the rider screamed, 'Varmint! Clear the way!' Strang met violence by reacting violently. No dumb animal charged at a clout. His fist balled, he bent swiftly, punching the horse's head with his gloved fist. The blow connected and Strang was almost unsaddled. Pain sped the length of his arm, but the injured horse, jerking up its head, turned sharply away, and reared on its hind feet. It was all the rider could do to keep saddle as the grey bucked and danced in a circle.

When his spooked animal was sufficiently quietened, the gentleman swung viciously on Strang. He was a man of about thirty, lavishly attired as if for a ball at court, and jerking on his reins and bending towards Strang, he abused him roundly, reaching for his cord whip as he did so. 'Dolt,' he snarled, 'you were almost the death of me. Clerks on horses are a hazard to gentlemen!' And so saying, he urged his nervous animal towards Strang and lifted his arm.

The tension left Strang and anger replaced the numbness he felt. It was the gallant's fault, he told himself, for coming on at break-neck pace in such a crowded area. Already other traffic – a coach or two, horsemen, and foot travellers – was gathering beyond them.

Strang had no intention of taking a whipping, or replying in kind. As the gentleman urged his horse forward to strike at him, cursing him the while, Strang unsheathed his sword and brought it up to protect himself.

It had an instant effect on the horseman. His anger was tempered by surprise, and surprise turned into black humour. 'What have we here? The clerk not only has a horse, but a sword too.'

A master now of the horse beneath him, he turned sharply and brought up his own sword in the same movement. Suddenly Strang was involved in a battle for his life, and hardly half hour in London. Rapier rasped against rapier, twice and thrice, with their movements made uncertain as their horses negotiated the lumpy cobbles beneath them. A crowd had gathered almost immediately and the scene was lit with naked torches and lanterns. Then suddenly two men pushed through the crowd. They were armed with pikes and lanterns, and were yelling at Strang and the stranger to stop.

A long pike was thrust between them and sharp quick voices – Strang had to get used yet to the rapid way people spoke in London – said they were under arrest. The word *arrest* had effect, especially on the stranger, who turned his anger onto the Watch. 'This is nonsense. I do but defend myself,' he shouted. 'This man blocked my path, pulled his sword upon me, and for all I know, might be a highwayman or an assassin. I am on my way hence to sup with King Charles.'

He added for good measure that he was Viscount Talbot, and the Watch readily and respectfully assured him that they recognised him as that Lord.

The officials now looked at Strang with suspicion. His travel-stained clothes, he was well aware, couldn't match Talbot's in splendour, nor in quality. Strang had come to London in a doublet made of leather with a heavy, roughspun black cloak such as clerks and priests might wear. But he told the Watch in a few brief words what had happened, adding, 'This Lord came from the side street yonder as if the hounds of Hell were nibbling at his horse's tail.'

The remark brought laughter from the crowd, and the Watch now asked him for his identity. Either he had told his story well or Lord Talbot was unpopular, for the Watch showed itself ready to debate the matter.

'I am Sir Harry Strang, fifth baronet, of Corsley, in the county of Oxfordshire,' he said.

Lord Talbot jeered in disbelief. 'A baronet dressed like a clerking scribbler? I think you should be held for investigation.'

'I'll decide who should be held, m'lord,' said the Watch.

'May I speak?' said a voice. A man in Quaker's habit had

stepped forward. In the light Strang saw black plain clothing and white shirt and the curiously shaped hat. 'I saw the incident,' said the man, 'and it was as this young man describes it. But only half the story has been told.'

At the invitation of the Watch, he told what he had seen. He seemed to be known and respected. There was a hint in the way he explained it that he did not care for Talbot. But Strang, thinking over the matter later, decided he might have imagined this because his evidence favoured him rather than Lord Talbot. His evidence was scrupulously fair. Strang had drawn sword first, he said, but only to defend himself from Talbot, who was about to lunge with a whip. Thus he was but defending himself, and, he hinted, 'Did a gentleman being attacked by another gentleman with a whip, reply with a whip?' There was a hint of sarcasm in his voice as if all gentlemen were beyond contempt and fighting, with whip or sword, was childish. His evidence that Talbot had spurred his horse from the lane at too fast a pace for safety and then demanded the safer passage along the wall, where people would almost certainly be travelling, clinched the matter in Strang's favour. The crowd looked angrily on Lord Talbot, for had he not collided with Strang he would almost certainly have hit somebody else, possibly a foot pedestrian, an old man or a woman, and caused them injury.

People began to shout at Talbot. They called him a fool, a drunkard, a criminal. One or two voices, lost in the crowd, managed to convey anti-royalist and republican sentiments in their accusations which told Strang that by no means everybody in London, as in country districts, had supported the return of the monarchy.

The Watch said he must take down names and report the fracas. Talbot angrily told him, 'Do what your simple conscience dictates, my man, and the devil take you.' He urged his horse forward, eyes lingering sardonically on Strang's plaincloth riding coat with the leather reinforcement at chest and elbows, and the thick dark roughcloth cloak which draped his shoulders. 'For your future, country baronet,' he sneered, 'I hope neither our paths nor our swords cross again.'

With that, he spurred off down the Strand in the direction of Whitehall, and after leaving his address in London with the Watch, Sir Harry Strang was permitted to travel in the opposite direction to Fleet Street.

It had taken much of the joy and thrill out of his first night in London and once again he was reminded of a nearby neighbour who had returned after a few weeks in London, seemingly struck dumb and morose, a changed fellow who hardly spoke.

On arrival at the King's Arms in Fleet Street, where his cousin, the Earl of Rochester, had instructed him to stay, Strang had sent a messenger with a note to Rochester's lodgings in Whitehall, and retired for the night. But bending from the window, with a new day bursting about him, Strang felt better. There was the wide variety of colours in the clothing of the people who passed beneath his window. There was much amusement and much life, and the girls were many. They seemed to be about in their very dozens, and what a contrast to his corner of Oxfordshire, where he might ride three miles with the intention of lying with some puddeny-faced country wench only to find three gallants there before him. This was the London of beautiful and willing women, a noisy place of intrigue, merrymaking, violence and love-making. He had already seen the rotting corpses of the footpads nearby Hyde Park. Yet Strang had seen only one hanged man before in his life.

He must steel himself to accept violence as a daily occurrence, and must remember only the good things London had to offer – money, position, power even; dancing, drinking, eating and wenching. Over yonder, just to the north, he knew that Smithfield lay. Many religious fanatics had been executed there by fire, and lustful Londoners, he had heard, still burnt the Pope in effigy there each year and to give the event realism and the necessary screams of pain, stuffed the dummy with live cats. Not far to the east would be the Tower where noblemen who offended the King could lose their heads. Further still, but to the north-west, would be the common execution place at Tyburn, where upwards of a dozen criminals at a time were publicly hanged. There would be pillorying and flogging through the streets. But if there was much death, there was also much life. While they had life, which they knew would be short, Londoners made the most of it. Taverns and eating houses would be on every street corner, vying with each other by attempting to offer better food and wine, and that would be something to see. There were the theatres and Strang had never seen a play staged; and there were crueller displays like animal fights and cock contests. It was a pity that there was only twenty-four hours in each day, only seven days in each week.

His spirits were already high with anticipation, as he turned from the window in answer to a knock on his door. Strang covered his bare shoulders with his cloak because of the early morning chill, and his spirits soared even higher when he saw the maid who brought a jug of steaming water into his room. Certainly no wench in a country inn was as handsome or finely dressed as this smiling, dark-eyed beauty. It only needed for her to be as willing as country inn wenches and London would become Heaven. She was expensively dressed. Her bodice, servant black, was of silk, and it fitted her slender frame with such care that it must have been cut by a tailor with a fine eye. Her smile of greeting was so warm that Strang, much to his consternation, found himself blushing.

Her movements were brisk and efficient and she had the manner of one who commanded authority. She looked at him with the same frank boldness as had the maid across the street earlier, and Strang guessed that this was a sophisticated city habit. In the country lasses by custom kept a distance and were wont to disguise their thoughts.

'Good morning, sir,' she said. 'I am Mistress Quick. I am sorry neither my husband nor I were on hand to greet you on your arrival. 'Tis said you are a kinsman to my Earl of Rochester but, if I may be so bold. I see not a family likeness.'

Strang smiled. 'Good morning. As for family likeness, I am but the country connection to the Wilmots. We are slow and dull and heavy, the Shire horses of the family.'

'Neither your appearance nor your wit suggests that to be true, sir.' She swept across the room, smiling as she came, and put down the jug of steaming water on the washstand. In the same fluid movement and with a rustling of lifted skirts, she had swept back the drapes of the four-poster bed and inspected the interior. A moment later she had turned and surveyed him with shock displayed on her saucy dark features.

She was inspecting the sheets and though her manner was merry, Strang felt some concern. 'Pray, sir, what is this? And you allowed here on the recommendation of my Lord of Rochester. Are you a drop-jawed Puritan, Sir Harry, that you sleep alone? If this intelligence goes abroad, I fear the King's Arms will lose its reputation and be ostracised by spirited stallions.'

Strang recovered himself and attempted to hide his embarrassment. That Rochester recommended him here should have told him all. It was unlike his cousin to nest at an inn for a night where he couldn't kill two birds with one stone, one in the kitchen for his stomach, one in bed for his comfort. He remembered on his arrival hearing much female laughter from the taproom.

'I see I must dress down the night porter, sir,' said Mistress Quick. 'And you on your first night in London. What ever can you think of us?'

Strang immediately claimed the blame, saying that he had arrived late and spent and had asked immediately for his chamber. He answered her saucy look by adding, 'A man shouldn't sup on fine bird unless he is sure he can do justice to the meal, lest his reputation be shattered.'

She nodded. 'Least, this way, sir, you will build suspense in the taproom, which isn't a bad thing.'

Strang wondered if the other female help in the King's Arms were as superb as this creature.

'Does the Earl of Rochester know of your arrival?' she next asked. 'I thought you were expected a month ago.'

'I was delayed. Your porter found me a messenger to send to my Lord of Rochester.'

She nodded. 'Perhaps it was good you delayed. Had you arrived a month ago, you would have found my Lord arrested and in the Tower – sent there by the King.'

It was Strang's turn to show concern and surprise.

Mistress Quick laughed. 'His crack-pated antics will get him beheaded before he is twenty and but for the amazing tolerance of King Charles, he would have been banished from the court if not the kingdom long ago.'

'Crack-pated?' Harry Strang said with disbelief. He knew his cousin to be wild and eccentric in his behaviour but he lacked neither intellect nor wit. Indeed he had graduated from Oxford University with a Master of Arts degree at fourteen, a record even if enemies did hint at collusion, and had already established himself as a scholar and poet, ranking as a poesifier beside John Dryden.

'If you have a care for your kinsman, Sir Harry,' she replied, 'you will plead with him to modify his ways. The King is undoubtedly his friend, yet not even he will always have the power to save him.'

'Why was he arrested, ma'am?'

She then told Strang how Rochester had been smitten by the wealthy Somerset heiress, Elizabeth Malet, but had had his suit rejected for his pains. Not to be thwarted, Rochester had played the highwayman one night and kidnapped her from the care of her grandfather, Lord Hawley. He had carried her off by another coach. Mistress Quick had a vivid imagination and painted a lurid scene. It was almost as if she had been there. Rochester had been about to launch himself upon the swooning gentlewoman, when the constables arrived. Lord Hawley had complained to the King and although, said Mistress Quick, it had been the King's idea that Rochester, who was penniless, should marry Lady Elizabeth Malet, he was forced to jail him. Rochester married Liz Malet three years later.

Mistress Quick bubbled on, for Rochester was a town hero. 'No sooner was he freed from this disgrace, Sir Harry, than he chanced his arm – although he often chanced something else – by penning a scurrilous poem about the King on the King's very door, where he was lying with the whore countess, Castlemaine.'

Strang found this hard to believe, but Mistress Quick not only said it was true but had memorised the poem, which was known all over town. She said it went:

'Here lies our sovereign lord the king,
Whose word no man relies on;
Who never said a foolish thing
And never did a wise one.'

Strang was horrified.

She saw that Strang found it hard to believe, and she smiled softly. 'I know the court very well, Sir Harry, and I know anything is possible there. As you will find out.'

'We hear stories in the country, ma'am, but we give little credence to them.'

'There you are wrong. Usually, one must wait until a monarch is dead before one hears the best – and the worst about him – but the King and Court and I are not strangers.' She laughed. 'But although King Charles is remarkably tolerant, I fear your cousin oversteps the mark.'

'I will tackle him on such behaviour, never fear.'

She turned to leave, again saw the empty bed; and again asked him to keep secret the arrangements of his sleep this last night.

Strang bowed. 'Your reputation, ma'am, never fear, is safe with me.'

'I'm glad to hear it, sir,' she smiled.

'Hear it well, ma'am, and believe it.'

'You are gallant, and I see the Wilmot touch in you now. I hope you will lodge awhile with us. We are more expensive than some, but you will find us worth the extra. Twenty-six pounds a year will bring you a fine chamber and full board.'

'It appeals to me, ma'am, but I must see what my kinsman has in mind for me.'

She bowed, left, and his spirits high, Strang turned to his toilet.

Chapter Two

SIR HARRY STRANG had breakfasted on cold mutton and ham washed down with ale before a commotion on the stairway and a loud thumping on the door of his chamber heralded the arrival of John Wilmot, 2nd Earl of Rochester. Wilmot had been the eldest son of his mother's second marriage to Sir Henry Wilmot, and had been born, as had Harry, on the estate at Ditchley, Oxfordshire. Sir Henry Wilmot had not fought as a Cavalier but after the King – then Prince Charles – had tried to retrieve the throne which had cost his father his head, Wilmot had enabled him to escape to the Continent after his defeat by Cromwell. It brought Wilmot an earldom and, after his death, a position at court for his son. Sir Harry's father, the fourth baronet called Strang, had died in battle against the Roundheads at the Battle of Bristol, where he had fortified his estate, and Cromwell had seized the Strang properties.

It was the Wilmot estates – by no means wealthy – that looked to the care of the Strang children, of which there were five, with Sir Harry the eldest.

The Earl of Rochester did not await the call, but came into the room as Harry rose from his seat by the leaded window to meet him. He was shocked by what he saw: The fine silken robe the young earl wore could not hide the debauchery which showed itself. Cousin Wilmot had always been slight and pale of complexion, and his fairness of hair made his features seem all the more wan. His eyes were bloodshot, his chin unshaven, and sleep and he were obviously strangers.

'Cousin!' Wilmot cried. They met and swung their arms about each other. 'A hundred apologies for my delay, but your message only reached me when I arrived home this morning.' He laughed.

Strang said it was he who should apologise for he had been late these past four weeks. But Wilmot shrugged this aside.

'The important point is that you are now here and away from

all country affairs and education and things. And that is good. Wisdom destroys happiness, and since the senses are the lights of nature, here comes Nan Quick with bottled wisdom.'

She was carrying two bottles of claret and she placed these beside the platters of mutton and ham. As she left, Rochester called her, mischieviously, not to wander off too far lest one of them have need of her private services. She closed the door, laughing.

'You like this place?' Wilmot said, yanking the cork from the nearest bottle. 'Nan Quick must be complimented on her enterprise. Once a gentleman booked into an inn, paid for a room he would not use, then went abroad at night, with all the danger that entailed, to find the nearest whorehouse. But along comes Mistress Quick and her ner'do'well husband and contrives to supply us with a tolerably good inn and bawdyhouse in one. It was an obvious thing to do, wouldn't you think, but it took a nimble-brained girl named Quick to do it.'

Strang laughed. 'I will neglect to write my mother that you booked me into a brothel.'

'Why should you tell her what she would already have guessed. If it wasn't would be the time to write her your complaint.'

Harry laughed. His kinsman might look ill-used but his ready wit suggested there was nothing drastically amiss with him.

'This place was called The King's Tavern in the times of the first Charles. During the dictatorship of the bastard Cromwell it tactfully became known as The Cock Tavern. Now it is the King's Arms but, methinks, since we know its uses, it should be called the King's Cock.'

Harry Strang didn't laugh, for the crude remark reminded him of what he had been told of his cousin's many indiscretions, in particular those directed at the king. Rochester, who missed nothing, smiled softly. 'It seems, cousin, that you have heard stories about me? Nan Quick lies often, but she speaks the truth. When I say she lies, I mean she lies at night, and has lied beside the king even. But she only lies a little, as prescribed by her sex, with her tongue.'

Harry poured himself a drink. He said, 'Cousin, this is no time for word games. There are family matters to discuss and, yes, the colour of your behaviour does trouble me.'

'You refer to the Malet matter. Cousin, I am an impatient man, and the fastest way to get a wife is to ruin her first. The dowry she will bring with her, incidentally, will hold off our ruin. Those damned Roundheads have left us little, and your branch of the family less. The King does what he can – bless him – but if he took back for all his followers that which was taken, it could lead to another Civil War. It matters not that we shall win this one, for Charles has the softest of hearts and baulks at bloodshed. Some say, 'Rochester added savagely, 'too soft a heart for he spared some of those who signed the death warrant of his father, the king.'

'The King is wise,' said Harry Strang. 'Why break open old wounds?'

'Perhaps,' said Rochester softly. 'The king is tired of violence, and yet we live in a violent age. And, me, I'm tired of life, and I'm not yet twenty.'

'Not yet twenty,' Strang replied, 'handsome, talented, titled, and held in high esteem at court. Why, you have many reasons to be happy.'

'To be happy, cousin, one must believe in something, yet all my instincts and observation force me to believe in nothing. Look about you at the evils and injustices of the world. And those people are the worst who promise us the best is yet to come – in the next world. Because you and I, Harry, know there is no other world than this.'

'You think too much and that is unwise.'

'And that's the wisest thing you have ever said. So an end to talk. Let's drink and shortly, why, Nan will come and we will come too.'

Rochester laughed, and the lines of fatigue fled from his face. His humour was infectious, and Harry Strang laughed too, and soon Rochester was laying out an itinerary for the day. First a call at the King's garment maker in the Strand. Following an hour in Braithwaite's to get Strang togged out fashionably for the court, a call to Knell's for a periwig, and then on to Whitehall, where Sir Harry Strang would be presented to the king.

But the plan was undone because the bottles were opened and then replaced by more. It was afternoon before Rochester suddenly became aware of the time. He had drunk twice as much as Harry and he had not slept or eaten. Strang was a little unsteady on his feet, but reasonably clear in his mind. Leaving the chamber, they almost fell down the stairs because of the darkness, and Mistress Quick, who met them at the bottom, avowed they were only worthy bait for bed and nothing else.

Rochester placed his arms about her and gently kneaded her bottom.

He chanted, 'My tail is for sale; just half a crown, brings me crashing down.'

'I fear the price has risen since you last made song here for your supper,' she responded.

'I forbid you to accept a peerage from the King,' Rochester told Strang, 'for the reckoning for peers goes double that for commoners. Fanny Pratt, of Drury Lane, has a notice between her breasts which says *Sleep where Rochester has slept,* but pays me not for the use of my name.'

Mistress Quick freed herself just as her husband, a tall thin man with a permanent landlord's smile, joined them, and this seemed enough to send Rochester hurrying for the street.

The mist had cleared and the day was warm, bringing up the smells from the gutter in the middle of the road. Strang wished he had left this member of his senses in Oxfordshire. He felt drunk but thought he could manage himself. Rochester was ahead of him, on runaway legs, scurrying towards the Strand. There were many people about but Rochester paid them little respect. He made straight for the wall, the safest place to walk, and defied anybody coming face on to him to battle with him who should step out to the road. Every now and then he yelled, 'Make way for peers of the realm.'

Strang kept close behind him, and caught most of the curses the pedestrians threw back at Rochester. Strang became concerned lest Rochester meet somebody with equal arrogance, as, say Lord Talbot, and rather than give way, both men were to go for their swords. Rochester, certainly, was in no condition to give a good account of himself.

Sure enough, as if thought had given birth to the incident, it happened, but with not the kind of opponent, fortunately, that Strang had expected. Rochester stopped, began to wave his arms and roar abuse. And stepping from the wall, Strang saw the man who blocked the way, and saw by his habit – black suit, white collar and cuffs and stove-pipe hat – that he was an elderly puritan.

He barred the way, made no reply to Rochester, but had lifted his old grey head in disdain.

'Out of my way, regicide,' Rochester snarled. 'I will not hesitate to kill a man who has killed a King. Give me not the excuse, Shaking Quaker.' He lifted his arm and demanded that he make way for a lord.

'I have right of way,' said the puritan sternly. 'I have but one Lord I submit to, John Wilmot, and he is not you.'

'By God's grace,' Rochester shouted, 'you will clear the way or contest me for it.' He snatched out his sword, but before he could raise it, Strang stepped forward and grasped the blade, forcing it down.

Strang was shocked. The man was elderly and unarmed, yet still Rochester, some fierce anger working in him, attempted to get away from his more thick-set cousin and lunge at the puritan. Now somebody else stepped forward, swiftly and dancingly, and stood in front of the old man.

There was a rustle of black dress, and suddenly Strang found himself looking at one of the loveliest of creatures. The plainness of her apparel, all black, with white cuffs, collar and hood-like hat, only seemed to add to her beauty for there was nothing on her to detract attention from her fine face, features, slim form, and her hands. Her hair was red, her lips bow-shaped, and her eyes sparkled now with anger and made them seem like green jewels.

'Put down your sword, sir', she demanded, 'before you disgrace yourself further.'

'Come, John,' Strang stammered.

But Rochester was fuming. 'If he fears to fight, this Prancing Quaker, why, then let his God fight for him. Order your God strike me down, regicide, before my sword strikes you.'

Strang now had Rochester by the arm, and Rochester was trying to turn away, and the incident took on comic overtones, although Strang could not appreciate them, when the old man started fighting with the girl. 'From my path, daughter,' he snapped; 'do not insult me by protecting me.'

This made Rochester's mood change abruptly and made Strang wonder if his cousin had not been jesting all along and did not intend to harm the man. For the puritan had pushed his daughter roughly aside, and Rochester now taxed him on this matter. 'Brute,' he declared, 'to so handle such a lovely creature. You puritans are all the same. Child-beaters, secret perverts, bullies, cheats.'

Then Rochester, transferring his sword to his left hand, stepped from the path, swept off his hat and, bowing, permitted the girl the path, saying, 'Ma'am, I extend you *my* pardon for *your* father's bad manners.'

The girl came forward, eyeing Rochester coldly, and Strang, also bowing, swept off his hat, but managed to look at the girl without trace of mockery. She looked at him once and then she had passed, followed by her father who grunted angrily and noisily.

Soon Rochester was off again, encouraged by either the laughter or the disgust of the crowd who had gathered, and now they were in the Strand, Strang for the first time in daylight, but there was little opportunity for him to see the fine houses in the stretch of road for Rochester, dicing with death, was skipping in and out among the fast-moving post-coach and horse traffic. Strang, panting hard, attempted to keep his cousin in sight and preserve his own limbs.

Another incident took place when Rochester, turning into Coal Hole Court, which he described as a short cut to the palace, ran ahead again, the intention to take Harry to a tailor and wig maker, apparently, forgotten.

In the narrow wind of Coal Hole Court, leading as it did sharply down to the river, they came across labourers constructing a house. They recognised the drunken and dishevelled Earl and called cheerful greeting to him because he was a famous wag about the town. Rochester could never resist an opportunity to take the stage and he stood in the court exchanging bawdiness with the men. Did such strenuous work, he wished to know, act upon a man as an aphrodisiac, or was it the reverse? Was a labouring man, after a hard day's toil, better between the sheets than a clerking fellow whose testicles had been resting on a high, hard stool the day-long? The labourers thought, in answer, that balls which had been dull in the day would be just as dull at night, and with this intelligence, which he promised to work into some verses, Rochester led the way along the court, waving in farewell.

He had not gone a dozen paces before, without warning from above, some kitchen wench emptied a pail of vegetable waste from a window three stories over their heads. Rochester got the worst of it. His wide-brimmed hat took turnip and cabbage leavings and his fine white feathered plumage became discoloured with vegetable stain.

Harry Strang, too late, jumped to the protection of the nearest building as over-ripe tomatoes splotched on the cobbles before him. He brushed peel from his arms as Rochester started to swear up at the window above. It had no use and, Strang presumed, the casement had been bumped closed as soon as the deed was done. But Rochester would have his revenge. He yelled to Harry to wait and ran back up the court and disappeared around the bend. Within a trice he was back carrying a house-builder's hammer and nails and before his cousin could guess at his plan, he began to nail up the front door of the nearest house. Strang stood watching him, and laughing, as he drove the long nails at an angle through the front door and into the jamp. When he had used five or six of the nails thus, he cuffed the sweat from his face with the ruffle at his sleeve and wanted to know why Strang still laughed. 'It is but a mean and weak revenge, cousin,' he said, offended.

'I laugh because it is the wrong house.'

Rochester swore savagely but brightened when he realised there were five or six more nails in the bag. 'The joke is on me,' he said, 'but now to correct it.'

Alternatively swearing, purple in the face with anger, then laughing at some huge jest, Rochester ferociously drove the remaining nails into the door jamp, firmly locking the inmates inside. The deed done, Rochester cheered his handywork, heaved the hammer aside, and then, taking Strang's arm, hurried him away to present him to King Charles.

Chapter Three

KING CHARLES was walking in the gardens at St James's when Rochester eventually found him. He had his dogs dancing about around him and several ladies and courtiers accompanied him. The King saw Rochester and Strang approaching across the green and turned to meet them, which surprised Harry Strang. He was to discover that the King found most court etiquette tiresome and was rarely one for pomp.

As the King approached, Strang was surprised to find how tall and well-shaped he was. He was better than six feet, like Harry was, stockily-built, and because his hair and eyes were dark was also of Harry Strang's colouring. The Stuart ancestry might be mainly Scottish, Strang reflected, but it was obvious there was French Bourbon and Italian de Medicini blood running in the King's veins. The King looked more at Strang than Rochester, making no attempt to hide his curiosity. There was a solemn, even brooding set to the King's swarthy features, and there was a sardonic touch, with mischief, in the smile with which he welcomed Rochester. It was a smile you would award to one with whom you had shared many disreputable moments and with whom you had secrets. The people who had accompanied the King, made no attempt to follow him, but meandered on their way through the gardens. But Strang was aware that he had occasioned curious glances and whispered remarks.

The King said, 'I came to meet you, my Lord, not to offer respect to your rank, but because the rank of your latest deed rankles with my ladies. No, don't protest your innocence. Mrs Thrain is a whore yet a whore is worthy of her hire and entitled to be proud of her calling. She can also be a lady.'

'Mrs Thrain?' said Rochester. 'I have offered her no offence. A lady or a whore – I treat them with like respect, for I know of no difference between them.'

'The difference is, I think,' said the King, 'that one must work for her daily bread.'

'Then, sire, we are all whores.'

'I won't bandy words with you, Rochester,' said the king sternly. 'You are irresponsible and indiscreet. Edward Progers is in position to do you much harm and I won't have my friends fighting among themselves. If Mrs Thrain said no to your advances, you should not let pride rule your pen or your prick.' He took a parchment from his sleeve. 'It is an amusing verse, if crude, but the point of the matter is that Mrs Thrain got the point and it gave point to her lungs which, as you will know, are as broad as her rump.'

'Mr Progers has shown you nothing but kindness,' the king continued after a pause, 'and I know this to be your work, even if the pen is disguised, because you were paying court to Mrs Thain and the give-away is in the title. I quote "To Her Who Refuses Just One." Since Mrs Thain uncrosses her legs only for Edward, both feel the insult sorely. And now I read,

'Her father gave her dildoes six;
Her mother made them up a score;
But she loves nought but living pricks,
And swears by God she'll frig no more.'

'How say you, sir? Do you recognise your work or have you to be drunker to recognise the smell?'

'My head is all wooden thick today, sire,' replied Rochester calmly, 'pray what is a dildo?'

The King did not enjoy the jest and there was an ugly pause. Strang was beginning to sweat. All his muscles seemed to ache and, quickly, Rochester complained, 'It was but tit for tat, sire. Mrs Thain did mock me over the Elizabeth Malet affair by saying that she couldn't play country games because she had lost her woods and mallet and did I have any suggestions. Since dildoes are wooden, the poem, at the time, seemed to have point.'

The King hid a smile. 'Just remember, John, that not all people have our wide humour. He looked at Strang now, and Rochester, again apologising, introduced them. Strang swept off his hat and bowed, and the King said. 'I'm not sure London has the stomach to accommodate two of your family simultaneously, Rochester.'

Rochester moved smoothly to the occasion. 'Then send Sir Harry to Paris as ambassador. Or what about those Dutchmen? He is strong, good with a sword, and will keep them respectful. My cousin is a fine soldier and sailor, sire, and like me he was trained to the sword by Draycott of York. If all other posts are full, we could send him to Ireland, however.'

The King ignored this bantering.

'Your father died at Bristol,' said the King. 'He was under my command in the west country. I knew of his worth though I didn't have the good fortune to have known him personally.' After Strang had thanked him, the King continued: 'Rochester says you are looking for a patron?'

'I am looking for employment, sire.'

'Employment?' the King was amused. 'Most callers are looking for a pension as if they are retiring before they have lived. Like Rochester here. How much is your pension, Rochester?'

Rochester smiled, ignoring the sting. 'You may call it pension, sir, since like most pensions it is little enough. But I, too, wait here to serve you – and in any capacity, and facing any dangers.'

'We know your worth, Rochester, especially as jester. The ladies know it the better. But, Sir Harry, you must realise the low state of my purse. Parliament – despite the fact I keep closing them down – won't give me the finances I need unless I beg. And I am a beggar who will not beg. They will have me keep the navy and army strong, and yet not strong, lest I use it against them. The money they do pay me, they accuse me of spending on whores.'

'Is there a better use for money?' Rochester interjected.

Beyond the King, just to his right, the courtiers had stopped and were playing with the spaniels. Strang couldn't help but notice the women. They were exquisitely dressed and stunning to look at and they moved and talked with an easy grace.

The King, ignoring Rochester, continued: 'Like many another great family, Sir Harry, yours has been made poor by fighting our cause. Nobody appreciates that more than I, and I am doing all I can but the task isn't easy.'

Strang felt hot and the implication, that he was begging, made him respond boldly, 'Sire, I seek no pension. Nor do I seek an easy sinecure. But I do seek employment suitable to what ability I might have, and this is for others to test and decide; and I do seek, earnestly, for a challenge against which to hazard any courage I might possess.'

The King showed pleasure, a pleasure tinged with caution. Perhaps, Strang reflected, he had heard such noble sentiments expressed too often before. But he said, 'You shall have employment against which to test your qualities, by and by. I think you will set a good example to your cousin who lingers too long at bottle and bed. A King always needs those about him whom he can trust, even if he does face difficulties in paying them. Rochester will seek his living on his back by marrying a heiress. Well, there's nothing at fault with that.'

Rochester interrupted, 'I'd much prefer a little privateering, sire, against the Hollanders and the French.'

'I have forbidden that – for the moment,' said the King. 'An heiress, especially a toothless one, would be less hazardous than piracy. But, Sir Harry, you strike me well. Rochester reads books and would work with his able mind, you seem the man who would prefer to read men and work with your hands. Perhaps General Monck could use you in the Army. But we must see. Please take lodgings in the city and attend me at court and, shortly, have discourse with Mr Progers.'

'Thank you, sire.'

'How much will you need for your expenses, Sir Harry?'

Strang hesitated, knowing not the cost of living in London, but Rochester answered quickly. 'I am on five hundred pounds a year and can scarce manage, sir. You could hardly give a kinsman less.'

'But your kinsman wishes to work, not play, and it is play, not work, which drinks up the money.'

'Very true, sire,' said Rochester with a lazy smile. 'But before a man may work he must needs acquire an education. There is much to London my cousin does not yet know but will cost him dearly to discover. Mistress Quick is attending to one side of his education. In the leave you have so kindly granted me, I will attend to the other. All it needs, sire, is for you to command me to send the reckoning to Mr Progers.'

'I granted you no leave from court, Rochester.'

'It was implicit in the anger you displayed. I thought a week of absence would be the better part of discretion.'

The King laughed. 'So be it. Sir Harry will have his pay. I'm not sure, Rochester, if you, with your glib and witty tongue, couldn't serve me best among my enemies – in Parliament.'

Rochester looked suitably shocked. 'Sire, would you condemn me to a profession which would stunt and twist me and make me a hypocrite?'

The King laughed. 'Play while you may, Rochester, for I have ambitious plans and you figure in them.' He tossed the piece of parchment containing Rochester's cruel poem about

Mrs Thain to the earl. 'I suggest you save your satire for the more deserving – and the more appreciative, John.'

Rochester caught the ball of paper. 'Thank you. A good rhyme is always worth using again.'

The two men bowed as the King turned, nodded to them both, and strode away. Then Rochester, hurrying at his usual breakneck speed, took Strang from the palace grounds.

Chapter Four

HARRY STRANG had been in London town hardly twenty hours and so much had happened and there was so much to see that he couldn't properly digest it or assess it. The noise and the smells horrified him, but since they seemed to trouble nobody else, he judged he must, in time, get used to them. Too many people crowded too closely together, was bound to effect standards. About the streets, he saw people relieving their bladder – and worse – against the nearest wall. Ladies and a few sensitive fellows appeared, when they received the call, to find a dark corner or an alley to attend their private business. The noise was accursed and, he thought, must eventually drive a body deaf. It was most horrible in the main streets like the Strand, where traffic became snarled and higgle-piggedly enmeshed. The iron-shod wheels on the egg-shaped cobbles gave off sounds like eternal thunder, and when you had a dozen such heavy coaches, all drawn by either four or six horses, the sound was out of this world and beyond the experience, he imagined, of any other.

But the smells which suddenly and unexpectedly smote one were crippling and Strang wondered if he would ever be immune. Rochester seemed most affected by the standards. Whenever he espied anybody misusing a wall, he would yell at them, 'I am the Earl of Rochester who will have a bill passed through Parliament making it criminal to piss, shit or gob in public.'

All he got was a puzzled stare as if the busy Londoner thought him mad.

But as they sped from the Palace of Whitehall, Strang's immediate concern was the madcap ways of his cousin. There seemed to be no ability to judge his own actions in Rochester, to know when he was going beyond the bounds of reasonable behaviour. His cousin's vulgarity with the King pointed to an over-familiarity which hinted at contempt and which, surely, the King was shrewd enough to notice. It was too early, however, for him to judge, for London behaviour was more informal and sophisticated than in the country. Nan Quick, who understood, had warned him, however, he remembered. He must watch his cousin carefully and evaluate before he could act.

But he could see already that cousin Rochester was overstepping the mark in his behaviour for he had seen him reprimanded by the King, and Mistress Quick had acquainted him with the fact that Rochester had already been incarcerated in the Tower, the imprisonment place for traitors. Then there had been the evidence of his own eyes, with Rochester challenging an elderly and unarmed religious zealot to a duel in the public streets, and the reckless manner he had shown when nailing the occupants of the two houses in Coal Hole Court into their homes.

And here was Rochester racing ahead, and on what mischief was he hellbent now?

Rochester led the way through the Stone Gallery, where the public promenaded or waited to see the King or his ministers, and was in such a hurry to begin that he would only wave to those gallants who attempted to speak to him. They crossed Whitehall and Rochester dived into an alley which bore the name Scotland Yard and turned into a yard which was a stable. A lad recognised him and, bouncing forward, bowed.

Rochester ordered two horses and Strang asked Rochester where they were going next. Rochester, telling him Drury Lane, explained: 'I am a patron of the theatre. I support the new innovation which has it that women should play female parts in plays. Formerly, boys were used. The puritans are against it, but they would ban the theatre anyway. But since it is new and there is no tradition and no school, cousin, good actresses are as rare in London as virgins.

'We have discovered a girl, however, who is a natural, and could be one of our greatest actresses. She is but fourteen, a slum child, and needs watching and protection. Her mother needs bullying lest she put the girl in a brothel, seeing no difference between whoring and acting, and the former much more profitable and secure.

'Now, cousin, when I received your message, I received another from this mother bawd. It makes mock of the English language, leaves much unsaid, but what do you think of it?'

He passed Strang the scruffy note, adding: 'This child is

particular to me for another reason, but that is another matter.'

Strang tried to read the illiterate scrawl but could make nothing of it and Rochester, impatiently, snatched it back, perused it, and said, 'It simply says, but not putting it simply, that some mishap has befallen Nell Gwynne, and if I still have her interests in my care, I will waste no time in getting to Drury Lane.'

Strang nodded: 'Then if you wish to go, John, let us go.'

Rochester was smiling at some memory. 'I am much impressed by this young girl. She's a cheeky imp. She met the King – you know. She told him that he must be an accomplished actor because, as a King, he was always on stage. She added, too, that she heard he never stopped performing, even when he was abed. The King was most taken with her and, fortunately, she is too young, as yet, for him to take.'

Strang smiled.

'Not bad for a child born in the rookeries, eh, cousin, but then her ancestry is good, in part.'

'Rookeries?' said Strang. 'What is a rookery?'

'The colloquial term for a noisy slum. The dwellers are packed so close together and make such a racket, that it is a reminder of a nest of rooks.'

The horses arrived. Strang, an expert, looked at them, and was satisfied. Rochester ordered the boy to charge it to his account – Strang was to discover that he lived perpetually on credit – and they mounted and rode into Whitehall. Rochester led the way into the square at Charing Cross, but instead of turning down into the Strand, took direction through St Martin's Lane, galloped through some alleys, and they came into some fields known as Long Acre. These were littered with rubbish and the bodies of either the dead or sleeping drunks.

Soon they were in another warren of alleys, closely-packed with evil-looking and smelling people, and now garrishly-painted women called to them from doorways and windows which were innocent of protective glass or board. Rochester did not stop until they turned into a slightly wider thoroughfare in which there were shops, taverns and eating houses, and Strang knew they were in Drury Lane.

Rochester turned northward, urging his horse through the press of people, who moved swiftly out of the way, and at the end of Old Drury, out beyond Holborn, Strang could see the fields and farms of the countryside, and imagine the sweet smells of fresh cut wheat, lavender, flowers and fruit. If a man be ambitious, he reflected, he must make some sacrifice. He wondered, however, if he would ever become accustomed to the rancid smell of close-packed humanity.

Rochester dismounted outside a half-timbered house which was more prepossesing than its neighbours and which carried a black bull sign. Rochester whistled an urchin and told him to mind the horses and Strang followed him into the tavern. It was dark and cool in the taproom and deserted at this early hour, and Strang judged from this that it was a tavern of the better sort.

'Have you any Northdown ale from Deal?' Rochester demanded.

The landlord apologised and stroked his portly belly.

'Damn,' Rochester cursed. 'Then make it Yorkshire ale–but let it be Yorkshire, mind.'

Rochester turned to his cousin. 'I have had thoughts about the message from the fine whore who is Nell's mother, and I see much method in the twaddle.'

The pots of ale arrived and Rochester wet his throat before continuing. 'The pox-ridden midden is frightened of me so I suspect she does not tell all the truth. I have a feeling, since it is customary, and Nell to my certain knowledge is a virgin, that the wench, who is as hungry for money as she is for cock, has sold young Nell to some wealthy reprobate, but he has not returned her within the specified time, and she is sorely troubled by it. With the note to me – and I am paying for Nell's keep – she shows her concern and, at the same time, absolves herself from blame. We will hear, I warrant it, a pretty story about how young Nell, with the urge high in her stomach, ran off with some randy rake.'

Strang did not know the people concerned, but he knew that Rochester, although young in years, was wise in experience, and could be close to the truth.

'This is the way, I think, the next act should be played, Harry. I would like you to visit the bawd first. She might say more to you since she is terrified of me. Pray you, say you are a work-mate of the poet John Dryden, who also has hopes for Nell, and who is sentimentally kind to hot-hen whores. I will call in minutes later and we will see if the cow changes her story for me.'

Harry Strang felt confused when he crossed Drury Lane to Old Bone Yard and to the house where Nell's mother, Eleanor Smith, had lodgings. He felt much was missing from the story and was puzzled why Rochester, whom he knew to be selfish, should concern himself about the welfare of a whore's daughter. But then, he was to discover, he hadn't met Nell. Before a day or so had gone, he would discover Rochester had two motives, and a third – and more astonishing motive – would present itself in a day or two. But immediately, he would discover that Rochester loved the theatre more than life itself and Nell Gwynne was a great character with a fantastic potential. The second reason was that Rochester, even at this early age, had begun to play politics. Nell's merry and original wit had already impressed the King. Nell, when she arrived, could help Rochester, who had helped her in both the theatre and the royal palace, for Rochester also had it at the back of his mind, knowing King Charles as intimately as he did, that he could manipulate Nell Gwynne into becoming a royal mistress.

Even knowing so little of the matter, Strang knew he must be on his guard because Rochester might get him embroiled in some mischief. A remark made by their maternal grandmother came to him down the years. She had said, 'John Wilmot is the brilliant one, but Harry Strang is the wisest.' It had always stuck in his mind because it had seemed to him a contradiction, for how could a person be brilliant yet not wise? The truth of the matter was now evident in Rochester's madcap activities and Strang must remember that he was the saner although not the cleverer, of the two of them.

Old Bone Yard was a narrow alley with fearsome smells and painted girls at the upper windows. 'M'lord, seek you a saddle?' called one. Strang ignored the call. The next woman, hearing the remark, called, 'I am a rider seeking a saddle, m'lord.' It seemed to Strang that the women had sensitive hearing attuned to the step of a man, for windows and doorways filled immediately. A serving woman called from the nearest doorway, 'Is you the Lord Meg Groome is expecting for a currycombing? Step this way and oblige.'

Mrs Smith's establishment, if the word wasn't inappropriate, was at the more respectable end of the alley, where both the houses and doxies, looked better preserved and more recently painted. A well-mannered maid conducted Strang to the rooms above, and Mrs Smith turned out to be a pleasing surprise. Although she must be at least thirty, since she had a fourteen-year-old daughter, Mrs Smith, with care, had contrived it so that she didn't look above twenty-five.

She yielded Strang a winning smile, and indicated a tray of

drinks. 'I have a taste for the new French drink introduced to the country, sir,' she said. 'Brandy. Would you join me in a glass?'

Strang said he would and liked the taste of it, but he felt compelled to say, before things got out of hand, 'I don't wish you to misinterpret the reason for my visit, ma'am. I call on behalf of a friend who knew I would be passing close by.'

She gave him a close scrutiny as if to say that she had heard this tale before and coercion or coaxing might be called for. Immediately however she pulled back some blinds and allowed more daylight into her quarters.

She had turned to face him, crossing the room in doing so, and she was now speared in the sunlight from the window. Strang noticed the discoloration on the side of her left cheek and two large bruises on her arm. She saw the startled look he gave and smiled, and said, 'My calling is not unlike that of a seafaring man's, sir. Periods of tranquil calm followed by storm, shot and much danger.'

'I'm sorry, ma'am. I meant not to pry.'

She smiled and waited, and then she said, 'Who is our mutual friend?'

'Why, ma'am, the poet John Dryden.'

'I see. A jolly lad.'

There was another silence, and Strang said, 'He asked me to call by and see how Nellie fares?'

'Nellie fares well. Please tell him.'

'She is not here? I hoped to see her.'

'Nellie is visiting with kinsfolk at Islington, a village a mile yonder.'

'I see.'

Strang felt that the initiative had already gone to the woman, and felt uncomfortable. She sensed that there was another motive for his visit but assumed, wrongly, that it was a nervousness on his part about coming to the point of his visit, sex. He spoke but his words seemed false, unnecessary, just delaying tactics, and finally he blurted out, 'Ma'am, when will Nell be back?'

When she answered him, her manner was casual, as if she too was aware of the fact that both of them were making conversation, the subject of which held neither of their interests. She contrived to move nearer to Strang as she spoke.

'Nell isn't needed back until the autumn theatre season, sir.

It is certain that then she will have her first part in a play, possibly with the Duke of York's Company.'

'I look forward to seeing it.'

She smiled, advanced suddenly towards him, and Strang made the mistake of getting up.

She would have thrown herself at him and Strang, cursing Rochester for being to long, said briskly, 'Ma'am, I must come to the real reason for my visit. My name is Sir Harry Strang . . .'

'Strang?' she looked surprised. 'I know the name well. I knew your father. But you are cousin . . .'

'To my Lord Rochester,' Strang interrupted, 'who sent me ahead. He is troubled by your note, ma'am, and will join us shortly.'

She dropped her professional poise immediately and adopted the pose of a stricken mother, a woman sorely used. 'Thank God my lord will act,' she stammered.

'Pray, ma'am, do not distress yourself. All will be put right. Please, seat yourself.'

She did so, touching at her cheeks to remove a tear or two which Strang decided to be genuine. She told her story then, beginning at the very beginning and keeping the point of the tale to the end, in the manner women usually use.

As Rochester had shrewdly judged, there was a man in the affair, but not in the exact manner he had suggested, nor with Mrs Smith's support – if she were telling the truth. She now maintained at great tearful length that she blamed herself for the tragedy, but how could she have known, when she first flirted with the famous Fighting Quaker, James Fox, that their turgid affair would release a sleeping tiger in the man. She had first seen Mr Fox preaching among the mullberry trees in Moorfields, she said, and had so been affected by the fire of him that she had returned over several weeks and made inquiries.

She found that Fox was regarded by many as a dangerous crank fit only for the rack and the rope, but they had become fast friends, and, as it does, one thing had led to another. Mr Fox, who was thirty-five, had never married. He had seen long and honourable service in the Commonwealth Army and even if Mrs Smith favoured the other side in the recent conflict, she was quick to realise that this didn't detract from Fox's manliness, for he had been in many battles and had been thrice wounded. He had reached the rank of captain and had received personal commendation from the Lord Protector Oliver Cromwell, himself.

Rumour had it – and this intrigued her – that Master Fox, despite his many years in the army, remained a virgin still. She had set out, she now admitted with shame, 'to seduce him to see if this was true. And,' she added as an after thought, 'to do Master Fox a service by revealing to the gallant gentleman another side of life.'

She had succeeded only too well, she admitted, and Master Fox had become a changed man. Like all Quakers he had been grim of face, she said, but now he became more morose and neglected to treat her with the gentlemanly respect he had shown her hitherto. Further acts of seduction had followed, for he came almost weekly to her house, but, she added once he had partaken of the well of love, his manner became obnoxious. He would insult her before he had recovered his strength sufficiently to leave.

The situation worsened to the point where Master Fox would strike her before leaving. 'Whore', she said, 'and devil's servant,' was the least of the names he had called her. Eventually she had sent Master Fox a note saying that he would never be welcome in her house again.

She continued, 'He did not answer this by post but three days ago, he called to the house with two strong friends, and while he held me, the two fellows with him bodily carried Nell away. Then Master Fox beat me – see my bruises – and said a whorehouse was no place to rear a child like Nell, who already had many wicked habits which he would shortly beat from her.'

'Three days ago,' said Strang. 'Last Sunday?'

'After his service,' she nodded. 'Since then I have become more worried by the hour. I remember things. For example, he was smitten by Nell's good looks and he is very manly in appearance and Nell, of late, has indicated that she is feeling fruity. Master Fox was always looking at her, and helping her with words, and still she hasn't returned.'

Strang found himself saying, 'With due respect, ma'am, many people would think a whorehouse no place to rear a child.'

Mrs Smith, agreeing the point, added: 'However, Nell is no child. She has the freedom of the streets and is far advanced in her years. Although she has a choice in profession, she had roundly declared that whoring is not for her. She is a warm child and feels the work too impersonal. All she has offered for sale, sir, is oranges in the theatre. Whoring might come yet, sir, for a woman in this world has but two professions – whoring and marriage, to marry one or lie with many, and there is little difference in it and it is a matter of taste – regularity or variety.'

'There is now a third – acting, ma'am?'

'Just another form of performing, but with clothes on – most of the time.'

'I see little harm coming to Mistress Nell whilst with Fox,' said Strang. 'He is your enemy, I must say, for you did him much harm by shattering his faith and making him feel unclean before the God he believes in. But I do not see him harming your daughter.'

She blushed, momentarily, and lowered her head and said, defensively, 'Do not scold me for I know that now. But he was such a sad-face, a drop-chin, that I thought he might peck-up if he got the taste. But what a strangely-twisted man he is, Sir Harry. I tell it badly, I see, for you are not convinced that Nell is in peril.'

Strang nodded. 'It is true men commit violence in the name of religion, ma'am.'

'Strange, sir, since they pray to the same God.'

'It is not religion which is wrong, ma'am, but man's interpretation of religious laws.'

'Religious preachers are as bad as legal preachers, Sir Harry. All are out to make a profit by confusing.'

Strang nodded, got up, and said, 'Damn, where is my Lord of Rochester?'

Mrs Smith had begun to weep again and Strang found himself embarrassed, and said, simply, 'I must assure you, ma'am, that Master Fox, although he did wrong in taking her, can mean Mistress Nell no harm.'

'I wish I could be sure of that,' she answered. 'My fears grow with the passing of time. He has seen much violence, and committed much, and do I now imagine the things he said, or did he actually say them? He became most violent when he was told of Nell's chances in the theatre, pacing the room madly, vilifying me and the theatre. He said the playhouse is the workshop of the devil and just another whorehouse.'

'A remark which makes him Rochester's enemy,' said Strang, and was disappointed because Mrs Smith missed the wit of it.

'When I told him about Nell's meeting with King Charles,

why he coloured visibly with rage and denounced the King in a most villainous and treasonous way.'

Strang looked at her swiftly and, embarrassed, misinterpreting his thought, she hastened to add, 'Perhaps I made too much of the brief meeting and the possibilities in it for the child.'

'Most folk do, ma'am,' Strang said, remembering his own recent meeting with the monarch, and his daydreams of what might stem from it and how, over the years, his account of their few brief words together might grow considerably in the retelling of it. 'You say he denounced the King?'

'Most viciously and vindictively.'

'What did he say?'

'The King was a religious intolerant . . .'

'Not true. He is possibly the only man in the kingdom who has tolerance for all denominations.'

'He said he was a Catholic and a supporter of the Pope.'

Strang hesitated. 'If he is, ma'am, he is a secret one.'

'And he claimed he was a king who was ruled by whores.'

Strang made no comment on that.

'I told him I prefer a man with vices and feared a man with none, Sir Harry, and I had my ears boxed for it.'

Strang nodded. 'You make sense, ma'am.' He was worried. Mrs Smith was obviously an intelligent woman, education or no. If she couldn't read books, her profession had taught her to read men, and what she knew about Fox made her fear the man.

'Master Fox,' she continued, 'was a violent man, but his violence was tempered by his faith. With what I did, I destroyed that faith and perhaps only the violence is left. Moreover, he hates the King. This I know. He was of the Fighting Quakers who attempted a revolution in London against the King soon after his crowning. Although he was not taken like the others, and was not suspected, he admitted as much to me.'

Strang said cautiously, 'There is something you haven't told me, ma'am.'

She admitted it at last. 'I gave Master Fox, in my anger, a more exaggerated account of Nell's meeting with the King than I should have done. I gave him the impression that there is some contract, er, understanding between the King and I, and Nell will visit the King to see if they suit in a year or so.'

'Runaway tongues can cause much mischief, ma'am,' said Strang. 'Where can Master Fox be found?'

Chapter Five

THREE things could hold Rochester away from his duties – wine, women, and an audience. He had been about to join Strang, he said defensively, when actors from a nearby theatre entered the Black Bull, and asked him for an opinion on Hamlet, which he gave at great length.

His eyes were more red-rimmed than earlier when Strang got back to the tavern, and he looked badly in need of rest; but he agreed that Master Fox was a dangerous man. 'He is a fanatic, cousin, and fanatics, fighting against insurmountable frustrations, are dangerous. Need for God's good grace, like need for wealth and power, makes men vicious.'

Strang ordered ale and they stood together in a dark corner. The boy outside still cared for the horses, sleeping in the sun on the cobbles, his back to the wall, the reins knotted about his legs.

Strang said, 'It's Mrs Smith's opinion that Fox has Nell Gwynne at his retreat – where he gathers with his friends – in a village called Kensington, a mile to the west of the city.'

Rochester nodded. 'I know the pox-ridden place well. A hideout for malcontents and where gentlemen who married money conceal their secret mistresses.'

Rochester was for riding to the village immediately, but Strang protested, thinking him not sufficiently sober for such a perilous venture, and this launched Rochester into further lecture.

'Fighting is but another form of violence like fucking, Harry; and it is the opinion of many that I do the latter supremely well, drunk or sober. Besides, a hard hour's ride, apart from making me randy, will clear the addle in my pate. We will go suitably armed and supported.'

They galloped to Rochester's lodgings in Whitehall. Although his pension of £500 made it impossible for him to run his own mansion, like other peers, Rochester lived in quiet, spacious and sumptuous luxury. He sent his man, Roberts, for fresh horses and two stout fellows to accompany them, and within the hour they were riding hard across the fields of Pimlico. Strang now had two heavy saddle pistols to hand and his rapier replaced by a trooper's broadsword, for Rochester said that Fox and his followers, all ex-Cromwellian soldiers, would be as heavily armed. Strang felt excited and a little concerned for it seemed he was riding into his first action. His concern was dampened by more concern, for Rochester treated the matter as lightly as he had the nailing of the doors in Coal Hole Court, riding madly, lolling and rolling in the saddle, singing, uttering war cries and, occasionally, freeing his sword and yelling for the charge as if the enemy already faced them.

Once they rested their horses and Rochester gave a vivid description lasting ten minutes of his part in the Battle of Naseby, to which they all listened with respectful care even though they knew he was old enough only to be at his mother's tits at the time.

Eventually they reached an inn on the outskirts of the village and Rochester went inside to seek information. Several people left the inn while Rochester was inside, and Strang noticed that one of them, as he mounted, looked them over carefully before he galloped fast away. Rochester appeared eventually and said, 'I fear we are in an Ironsiders stronghold. Master Fox is much respected in these parts for the bastard had committed many kindnesses.'

Although the landlord of the Bunch of Grapes had respectfully answered Rochester's questions, he had let everybody in the room know after whom Rochester was inquiring, and Strang told his cousin of the man who had paid them some attention before galloping away.

'The readier they are, the better the battle will be,' Rochester observed, and led the party to the house at the other end of the village.

The house was hidden by a quickset hedge which had been allowed to overgrow. The house was an early Tudor structure of two floors. 'No doubt built by some corrupter on the profits made from those stupid Welsh kings,' Rochester observed.

They sat horse at the gate. The place looked empty. Nothing stirred. The pathway was overgrown, the garden weed-choked, which brought Rochester into criticism again against lazy Quakery.

They made plans for the attack. Rochester and Strang would approach the house from the rear; the three servants from the front, but only after Rochester or Strang called to them or had made entry to the house.

Then Rochester suggested that the party not hesitate, but use their pistols on the first opportunity, and this brought him into conflict immediately with Strang.

'You are an innocent, cousin,' Rochester protested; 'you know not these mad people. They are but fanatics who will thank you if you help speed them to Heaven. The King is behind us, never fear, and I will have a back-dated warrant for Fox's arrest tomorrow to prove it.'

'I say we not show violence until it is first shown to us,' Strang answered hotly.

Rochester turned truculent. What added to his annoyance, he explained later, was that Strang argued in front of his servants who might themselves have doubts about shooting at Quakers.

'You are a fool, cousin, and hardly in London long enough to know the wickedness here.'

Strang said manfully, 'I suggest that I go to the house first and ask them to give up Mistress Nell.'

'I forbid you, cousin, to commit suicide,' Rochester said hotly. 'You are a country bumpkin, sir, and you know not the savagery in these people.'

Roberts interrupted, 'Forgive me, sir, but my Lord is right. These are desperate fellows and will not hesitate to show us violence.'

The other two men added their agreement to Roberts, and Strang, reluctantly, found himself giving way.

'Right,' Rochester snapped loudly, 'enough time has been wasted. Shoot on sight to maim and kill.' He glowered at Strang. 'The mother whore has much to answer for. You do not see it, cousin. But these scoundrels be out to get at the King.'

After repeating the instructions in a loud and angry voice, Rochester gestured impatiently at Strang, and turned to a meadow at the right of the house.

The sun was fading as they found a break in the hedge and tramped up slope through the high grass, Rochester pushing ahead, stamping the ground, the anger still with him. Strang was troubled. Rochester and the others were convinced about the need to use violence first, and debate later, but were they right? Their cause might be just, to release Nell Gwynne and return her to her mother, but then Fox might readily argue that he had rescued her from a vile place. Yet Strang was demanded that he shoot first. He felt that he was being pressured into some business which was not entirely correct.

They ploughed through the long grass as an orange sun sank over the hill, and all was peace and quiet about them. They came on a young couple, wrestling in the grass, and the encounter put Rochester in a better mood. She was in the smock of a milk maid and the boy the uniform of a groom, and they pretended to be fighting over the ownership of a bucket which they had gripped between them. The girl was giggling, with her long skirt flying, showing her white cotton hose.

Rochester grinned, smirked back at Strang, and paused to survey the scene, and then gave off one of his famous impromptu verses.

He sang:

'Jack and Jill
Went up the hill
To fetch a pail of water
Jill came down
With half-a-crown
But not for carrying water.'

The couple, frightened, released the bucket, and would have scampered away; but Strang swiftly reassured them. He told them not to be frightened, they meant them no harm, and they were on the King's business and going elsewhere.

'Nor do you, my lass, have anything to fear from that buck,' Rochester told the girl. 'Perhaps I should dally and show him how.'

Strang urged Rochester on as he himself hurried past the couple. Rochester laughed and, in good spirits, followed him. Strang looked back at the girl and something about her, perhaps her frank look or apparent innocence, reminded him of the girl he had seen that morning in the Strand when Rochester had picked a quarrel with her father. This girl was a blonde; the other had been red of hair, but that was the only difference, it seemed.

Eventually they reached a rear gate in the hedge, and it was while they inspected the house from there, that the violence erupted. It was so sudden and so alien to the pastoral scene, that shock put pain through Strang's body. Rochester punched him immediately and they both dropped together. Strang had vaguely seen a shadowy figure by the door, seen a flash of flame, and a ball tore twigs from the hedge beside them.

From cover, Strang called for a parley, but this was ignored.

Rochester mocked them – probably deliberately. 'Were he alive, you rotten shots, Cromwell would have your balls for wasting balls.'

'You be the devil's man, Rochester,' came a voice. 'There be nothing here for you but death, sir.'

'I see the bastard now,' said Rochester. He poked a pistol through the staves in the gate, and fired. Strang heard a musket clatter to the ground. A blackcurrant bush jerked violently and a man crashed down beside it.

Another shot rang out. Twigs and leaf splayed around Strang's head, and he detected movement at the window above. Strang also noticed that the back door was ajar and a man stood almost hidden there, with a musket.

The man waited and, uneasily, Strang waited. Neither was an easy target for the other and Strang felt, nervously, that the man was waiting for the attackers to show themselves. Rochester was in a hurry to be inside. He pressed hard at the gate to see if it had fastening, which it did, halfway up the gate, and it was Strang who raised himself and shook it loose.

Rochester had abandoned his empty pistol. He now carried his sword and the remaining pistol and he looked questioningly at Strang, indicating the house.

Strang tried once more for negotiation. He called that they came in peace to secure the release of Nell Gwynne, and if she was released into their care, they would leave immediately. There was no answer and Rochester told him, angrily that he was wasting his breath. 'We hit them now,' he added; 'they have but muskets, clumsy instruments, for close in work.'

Strang decided to go through the gate first and Rochester would cover him. He leapt through the gate, dived to the ground, and since nobody fired at him, he hoped the defenders had come to their senses.

Rochester took heart from the silence, and tried for peace. He called: 'Listen there, I am John Wilmot, Earl of Rochester, on business for the King. I want nought from you but the maid, Gwynne, placed into my safe keeping. Refuse me and it will lead to violence, and violence could bring you all to the gallows.'

The silence continued, and angered by the lack of a response, Rochester called to Strang to be on watch because he was coming through the gate. He entered the vegetable garden foolishly and without the speed and care shown by Strang; and perhaps because of this, or because he was the hated Earl of Rochester, the man in the upper storey fired his musket.

Rochester yelped and fell and, believing him mortally hit, Strang rushed the man at the open door, firing his pistol, levelled at lock height, from some ten feet away as he came. The shot was neatly timed and placed. The ball clipped splinters from the door but kept its path and caught the defender. Strang reached the door as the musket drooped and kicked it in. He had already abandoned his empty pistol, and now unsheathed his sword.

By throwing in the door, Strang propelled the wounded man back. He fell heavily, sprawling in the passageway, with his hands plunged against his wounded side. Blood shone in the darkness, bubbling up through his thrashing fingers. The man was in great pain and Strang wondered if he was about to die. All Strang's muscles now seemed to be taut to breaking point and gave him pain. He heard a burst of shots from far off and decided Roberts and the other two men must be assaulting the front of the house. But how many defenders were there? he wondered.

He dropped after stepping carefully over the wounded man, crawled along the corridor, listening carefully. No sounds now came from the front of the house. Behind him, as if praying, the wounded man whispered to himself. Strang felt a moment of nausea and vomit came into his throat. He reached a staircase and peered up it. The man with the musket who had dropped his cousin would be up there, and he alone had to deal with him. He would be desperate. He had heard Rochester give his name and say he was on the King's business. Since he couldn't save himself, the man might well fight to the death against those he saw as God's enemies.

Strang had an immediate vision, which he strived quickly to repel, of a family conference discussing his violent end in less than twenty-four hours after his arrival in London. He could see each of his relatives and saw each of them speak, and knew, by their characters, what they would say. But he moved to the staircase, standing, to climb it, because Rochester, who had fallen, would have wished it and must be revenged, and then Rochester spoke to him. Strang turned and saw his cousin step through the door, taking care to avoid the wounded man.

'John?' said Strang. 'Are you not hit?'

'Hit but not hurt,' he said cheerfully. He ran to catch up with Strang, and beat him to negotiating the stairs. 'Let's clear out this gallows-bait and burn their rat-trap,' he said.

Rochester charged up the stairs, not bothering to take cover, and Strang could do nothing other than follow him, his remaining pistol lifted at the ready. Because of the upstairs windows, the landing was better lit. There was only one man in this section of house and he was waiting for them, a short, squat-shaped man with black shaggy hair and a defiant manner. His expression suggested blind and implacable hatred towards them, not fear. He was old, perhaps forty, but muscular and well-preserved, and he carried a heavy broadsword such as would be issued to troopers in the Cromwellian Army, and he looked as if he had its measure and his handling of it.

'Stay apart, Harry,' Rochester said fiercely, 'this man is mine.'

'I seek no favours from the devil,' the man snarled. 'The two of you and it's all the same to me.'

'I will not have you telling them in Heaven, brother, that John Wilmot didn't give you equal chance. Which is more than your deserts. But, there, I'm a sporting man.'

They faced each other on the landing with but six feet between them and, since there wasn't room for him, Strang stayed on the stairs.

There was no sounds of firing from the front of the house now, but Strang contrived to watch below and beyond the ex-soldier in case his cronies came to his aid.

The soldier attacked first, perhaps thinking he had caught Rochester off his guard. There was a vicious sheen in his eyes, his lips curled his contempt, and he yelled, 'Death for the royalists,' which was possibly his old troop's battle cry, and lunged. Rochester took the blow on the side of his sword and metal scraped as he dragged his sword away. 'Here is a dunderhead, cousin, who hasn't heard the wars are long over, and that a King is back.'

He lunged again, bringing over his sword with as much power as he could muster, and there was a clank as steel met steel, Rochester was taller but lighter. But the soldier, if he had width and weight on his side, was smaller and older. Rochester had superiority in skill, having been trained by a master, but it was an art which he could not use. The rapier had been abandoned for the chopping broadsword of the battlefield; moreover, there was no space for fancy footwork and crafty subterfuge. It would be a chop-at and hammer-at slamming match with brawn, not brain, pointing to the winner. It gave the old soldier a more equal chance.

There were a dozen swift and heavy blows from the man. Strang could see the perspiration on his face and the desperation and hatred there. He was fighting for his life and he had hatred also supplying him with power. Rochester was put on the defensive, although holding ground, and resisting the blows easily enough, though Strang couldn't see his face and didn't know whether he was tiring or not. He knew that Rochester had been drinking heavily for some twenty hours at least and had gone without sleep the night before. But Strang, honour bound, could not go to his aid.

Then Strang heard running footsteps below and lifted pistol and sword at the ready. He saw Roberts first, an anxious, sweating Roberts.

'It is over, my Lord,' Roberts said excitedly. 'They have surrendered at the front and are disarmed. Mistress Gwynne is in a room up there.'

Strang yelled the news to Rochester, the swords clanged together once more, and then Strang shouted at the man, 'Put up your sword. It is finished. We offer you your life.'

The man stepped back, warily, sword still lifted. Roberts repeated the news as he came thundering up the stairs.

'If we are free to go,' said the man watchfully, 'I will not fight.'

'You are free,' said Rochester. He was red in the face and reaching for his breath. 'But another matter is whether Fox should face trial as a kidnapper.'

Roberts interjected, 'My Lord, the preacher is away. He is said to be in the Shoreditch area.'

'Let us see if the girl has been harmed,' said Strang, 'before we decide that.'

Rochester smirked ruefully, 'If you knew Nell, the more harm, the better.' He sheathed his sword and the ex-soldier dropped his on the floor. 'You know nought about religion,' Rochester told him, 'but you caper with a sword convincingly.' He asked him where Nell Gwynne was kept, and thc man indicated the corridor.

Rochester and Strang hurried along it. Rochester called her name several times.

Eventually a girl answered them from a room in a matter of fact tone which, if anything, implied amusement. 'I am here. Alas, I am not yet ruined but I have been sorely used.' Her voice was chirpy, melodious, cockney.

Rochester turned a key in a rusty lock and they came face to face with Nell. She waited for them in the middle of the room, barefooted and dressed only in a short cotton shift that barely reached her thighs. If Strang was a little disappointed because she wasn't as beautiful as he had been expecting, he soon forgot this under the spell of her bubbling, impish personality.

For, at first glance, Nell was just another pretty face, with bronze-gold hair, deep blue eyes, pouting lips, and a fragile-textured whitish skin. But when she smiled, which was often, two dimples showed in her cheeks.

'Why,' she murmured with amusement, 'here are my saviours, and my Lord Rochester in the van, my very own Lord Protector. Do you wish for your reward now, sir knight, or will you take me up firmly later on the matter?'

Rochester answered her in a bantering yet rough manner. It was as if he often found himself in conflict with her or impatient with her activities. There was even a touch of paternalism, Strang was to discover, in his manner to her, which he found surprising coming from Rochester.

'We are on a serious matter and blood has been spilt,' Rochester said, 'so watch your tongue. You are not too old for a thrashing.'

She smiled and the dimples showed. 'Why, sir, I have had that – the thrashing. Look you.' She lifted her shift. Since only a few women in England, those usually ladies at court, had adopted the French female habit of wearing drawers, Nell's buttocks and thighs were naked. Turning from them, she hawked forward, the better for them to see her buttocks. They saw the marks on her soft and rounded flesh.

'Who did that?' Rochester demanded. His voice lacked anger.

'Is that envy in your voice, my Lord?' responded Nell. 'It was Preacher Fox. He said a beating would be good for my soul. I corrected "arsehole", and promptly got a repeat performance.'

Rochester inspected the damage, his fingers lightly brushing the bruised flesh. 'What think you, cousin? Is it a serious matter?'

'No more, surely, than whores in the Bridewell Prison receive as rations,' said Nell.

Strang, hiding a smile, inspected Nell's buttocks. 'Well, the skin isn't broken, John.'

Nell gave him a cheerful smile, studying him closely as she bent, and said, 'Help yourself, sir, since Lord Rochester is.'

Just then they heard somebody hurrying up the stairs at the end of the corridor, there was a conversation, then Roberts appeared. He had sent one of the men to look at their horses and whilst in the road he had seen people approaching from the village. There was a great many of them, judging by the lanterns and the torches they carried.

'This isn't a safe place for cavaliers,' said Rochester. He slapped Nell's bottom, reached for a cot blanket, and tossed it roughly over her shoulders. Then he asked Roberts about the fighting. Roberts said one of their men had been slightly wounded, as had Rochester himself. Three of the defenders had been wounded, and it was thought one would die shortly, and Rochester counselled that they leave immediately.

When they got to the horses, they saw more than a score of lights flickering down the road. They mounted, with Rochester calling that they ride away through the darkness in the opposite direction.

Nell rode behind Rochester, who led the way. She straddled the horse behind Rochester, and since she had to hold to him with both hands, she lost her blanket when he put his horse to the gallop. Strang galloped close behind and watched in the darkness as the girl's short shirt danced in the wind. But there was not a lot to see. The sky had clouded and there was neither moon nor stars.

Chapter Six

EVEN though the cheerful landlord at Notting Hill Barnes had a full house, he maintained that nobody was ever turned away, though, with a grin, he doubted whether he could promise them single beds and chambers – not that he expected anybody wished that. 'All you can eat and drink for a shilling a head, my lords,' he said.

They dismounted in the busy courtyard, and the landlord, seeing the almost bare Nell, allowed his imagination to tell him what had transpired between five men and a bare-bottomed lass. Nell decided to have sport with him. Affecting a refined voice, she said, 'I was kidnapped, sir. These are my brave rescuers. Why look, I was beaten within a fraction of death.' She turned and showed him her bruised flesh. The landlord responded melodramatically, hands lifted, eyes shining, mouth gaping with horror. 'What is the world coming to, sirs?' he demanded. 'Not a day passes but I hear a like story. It is no longer safe for Christian people to go to their beds alone.'

'Nor is it wise that they should,' Nell interjected mischievously.

The play actor in Rochester made him respond. 'My good man, it was hot while it lasted, but it is over now. I have a slight flesh wound.' He lifted his cloak. 'More damage to a fine coat, however, than Wilmot flesh. I will have poultice and bandage for my arm, the lady's rump, and another of my stalwarts is slightly wounded.'

'But of course! This is terrible. At once.' The landlord's hands still dramatically cut at air.

'Incidentally,' Rochester said languidly. 'I am John Wilmot, Earl of Rochester. This, my kinsman, Sir Harry Strang. The lady, as a matter of discretion, will remain nameless, you understand. Nothing about this to anybody. We are on the King's errand.'

The landlord became speechless.

'I need your best chambers, sir,' Rochester continued. 'The

very best, mark you, for myself, my friends, my charge, and my servants.'

Promising Rochester all he wished, the landlord led them into the huge room of The Rising Sun Tavern. The cooking fires stretched the length of one wall, and all types of meats and poultry was roasting on spits. There were tables of fresh bread, fruits, vegetables, wines and beers. Perspiring servant wenches hurried along the fireplace basting meats and fish, and checking that vegetables were not burning. The landlord cleared idlers away from the best table and found two of the serving wenches, selecting the most attractive, to wait on their table. The word that the Earl of Rochester was there soon got around however, and people found excuse to pass the table. Rochester, accustomed to being a celebrity, ignored this. 'After the great victory,' he told Strang, 'the great drunk.'

Jugs of wine and ale arrived, followed by shell fish and cheeses and hot bread. With a mug in his hand and an audience before him, Rochester was soon dominating all. Nell had been forced to sit on Strang's left, who was on Rochester's left, and found herself out of the conversation. She wanted to discuss Fox and her rescue, but Rochester seemed to be bored by that subject.

Rochester had attracted the attention of the two girls sent to wait on their table and he was talking a lot of nonsense so to impress them. This consisted of banalities about the court and the King's name – what Charles had said to Rochester, or Rochester to Charles – was often used. Eventually Rochester told the two wenches that they were so evenly matched that he couldn't decide which one he would sleep with that night, and suggested they toss a coin and decide the winner. He added, gallantly, he would return another night to service the loser.

Strang was to find, on this occasion, as on others, that Rochester's behaviour brought him acute embarrassment, for he was often boastful, transparently conceited, offering stupid remarks or obvious lies. What was remarkable, however, was that nobody except Strang seemed to mind. The girls laughed at Rochester's news and then, slapping Strang's shoulder, Rochester said, 'But here is the booby prize. A lusty lad fresh from the country. What say the loser to him?'

The girls, who were already embracing Strang in their hot looks, giggled again, giving their acceptance without the immodesty of putting it in plain words.

Strang, with a mouthful of lobster and French wine, could

only agree with a wink, and Nell Gwynne, liking not the conversation, demanded Strang's attention, as wolfing into fresh salmon, she gave him a long account of her many troubles and worries. But, as always, she larded her talk with a satirical edge. Strang would eventually think of her as an actress who was always playing a part in some imaginary play, but one who was capable of laughing at herself as well as at others. She was drinking heavily, too, and she was soon looking at him with a song in her eyes as her lips danced.

She became bitchy about the serving wenches. One was flat-breasted, she observed, the other thin. She begged Strang not to lie with either of them for she knew a woman with the Spanish Pox when she saw one. Later she demanded from Strang whether or not he found her beautiful and, with a mouthful of venison, Strang could only mumble the fact that he did. This brought a demand to know why Rochester had refused to swive with her. Strang gagged on a mouthful of food, but managed to recover sufficiently when he had cleared his mouth to tell her that Rochester had scruples. 'You must need be patient, Nell, for you are too young.'

'What had age to do with randiness?' she demanded, and then complained about Rochester's manner to her. She told Strang of a snide response Rochester gave when she had met with the King. The King had told her, 'Mmm, pretty wit.' And Rochester had sneeringly interjected, 'Pretty? Shit!' Strang explained it away by saying that his kinsman would reach any lengths for a pun and she shouldn't take it as meant.

He added, the drink already taking a hold, 'You are the prettiest and wittiest girl in this room.'

Nell sighed. 'If that be so, it is strange, for I am surrounded by the most ball-less of men. Rochester won't, Fox don't. And what about you?'

'When I can, I do, but, ma'am, not with you.'

'Another fucking poet,' Nell said. 'And what do you mean "When you can"?'

Strang explained that living in the country, where population was sparse, raised certain problems. He hurried to mollify her by saying: 'But I agree, age should have nothing to do with it. A girl is ready when she is ready, whatever her age, and this can be read in her face when she looks at you.'

'Then, Sir Harry,' she affected maiden modesty, 'I am in reach and I am ready.'

Strang did not answer and Nell, nudging him with her naked

thigh, added, 'Turn, sir, look at me in the eyes and see that it is definitely so.'

'It is so, but with us, ma'am, it is not definite. Nothing personal but your age is against it. If Rochester won't, I won't. Now let me get drunk in peace, sweet Nell.'

'Now I will get drunk,' she said angrily, reaching for the wine jug, 'and I will shortly lie with one of the stable boys, but, mark me, not the shortest.'

Strang waited until she had filled her mug then held his own out for replenishment.

She did this and her anger held in, said, 'You didn't hear me, m'lord. I will swive with the horniest of the stable boys. And what a way to return me safely to my mother, sir, with hay in my hair and corns on my arse.'

'Eat, drink, Nell, and shut up.' Strang had caught the eye of one of the serving wenches who hovered about the table now.

'I have you summed up right, Sir Harry,' said Nell. 'At first I thought you better quality than my Lord of Rochester, who has all devices to keep me from his bed. You, sir, are as ambitiou as your cousin. My Lord of Rochester, along with my whorish mother, thinks he can preserve me for the King and in so doing preserve his own position at court. The King likes me, it is said, and waits. Well, he is a fine man, and a King with it, and I am willing but I'm fed up with waiting. And a girl, like a horse, needs exercise and practise. And if neither you nor Rochester will make effort to please me, you'll rue it when I get to court.'

'You have the desire, Nell,' answered Strang, 'but it could be, look you, a false dawn. A premature summer, it seems to me, and you won't like the storm.'

'You, sir,' she flared, 'begin to sound like Preacher Fox, another non-starter in sexual matters.'

Although the sweetness of Nell's nature managed to take some of the sting from her words and make them, at times, seem almost playful, Strang could detect the determination behind them.

'Ah, now the truth shows,' he answered lightly. 'You tried your tricks with Master Fox – that got you the beating. Good for Preacher Fox. We have done him an injustice.'

He reached across the table for a turkey wing, coming close to Rochester as he did so, and suggested, as Rochester turned to smile at him, that they invite the two serving wenches to join them at table, since they were short on female company.

'Nell is driving you hard, eh, cousin? It is arranged. They will join us shortly – for the main course.'

Strang attempted to placate Nell by giving her the piece of turkey. She took it, but kept up the pressure against him, with her thighs and her mischievious words.

'It is not good to eat and talk,' Strang said, lifting a whole pullet onto his plate.

Nell, ignoring this, said, 'The ladies at court call King Charles "Old Rowley" which is the name of his stallion. Have you heard this?'

Strang, grunting, said he had and not yet knowing what was coming, was pleased that the subject had been changed.

'It is true,' she added, 'and so it is said that your cousin, my Lord Rochester, is frightened to lay with any lady with whom the King has laid, or is likely to lay with, because he doesn't want to come second in any comparisons of size and performance.'

Strang became angry. 'You show an ill grace, Nell,' he protested. 'My cousin has many faults, he is often cruel, but he has shown you – which is perhaps unusual for him – only kindness, courage and protective affection.'

Nell giggled, and Strang saw that she was but testing him.

He added lamely, 'And having shared several country wenches with my cousin when we were in our early teens, I have knowledge that he is well equipped and has the stamina.'

Nell snuggled up to him as she drained her mug. 'I like you when you are angry, Sir Harry. And I enjoyed your confession. But if you started at fourteen or fifteen, why shouldn't I?'

'It's different for girls.'

'And I will let you into a secret. I think you are handsomer than your cousin. He has the title, the clothes, perhaps the money, but you attract the most. You are solid and serious, but not without a ready sort of humour.'

'I'm but a plain and ordinary man,' Strang said, but he was delighted.

'And that's the way many girls will have it, sir.'

'You are an expert, to be sure, at fourteen, Nell.'

'And when I'm fifteen you shall swive with me.'

'It is agreed.'

'I am fifteen, yesterday, sir,' she laughed; 'and cannot remain a virgin still.'

'This must be checked out with your mother.'

'All right,' she answered him brightly, 'I am not yet fifteen.

A girl now, but shortly a woman, by courtesy of Sir Harry Strang.'

The eating house was unusually packed and they discovered the reason from the landlord. He told them there was to be a bear fight, and would like to know if they wished choice seats saved. Rochester said he needed quieter sport, and would the landlord send the wenches to join them. This the landlord said he would do presently.

Nell turned on Rochester. 'I see my lord, that I am to be neglected for these whores. I'm neither baby nor toothless crone. Nor will I be shelved for the pleasure of the King.'

Rochester grinned. 'You put too much store in the King's glance, Nell. I fear you might be disappointed in your hopes. The King, since he likes them much, smiles on all comely women, be they toothless or babes.'

'So you say now,' she answered.

'You have a rarer talent, Nell,' said Rochester, 'and the playhouse is to be your lover.'

'I would rather fuck a man than the theatre, m'lord.'

'Your name, Nell,' said Rochester, carried away, 'will be known long after you are gone. Think of that.'

'I think that I'd rather be warm in my bed than famous in my grave. And so tonight, m'lord, I will share sheets with Sir Harry here, who is most handsome.'

Rochester shrugged. 'It shouldn't affect your acting. But that's up to Sir Harry. But, I warrant, he prefers yonder tiny blonde.'

'This we will see by the effect I have,' said Nell, and she swung suddenly, discarded the cloak the landlord had earlier sent her, and dropped onto Strang's lap. She placed her arms about Strang's neck and began to wriggle herself into a comfortable position on his legs. Strang could only remove her by using rough methods, for she clung to him with the persistence of a leech. Other revellers noticed it and began to call encouragement, and a natural actress, ever ready to respond at the appearance of an audience, Nell began to play a part.

Since he couldn't be rough to her, Strang could do nothing else but sit still and let her wriggle about on his lap, and, frowning as if puzzled by something of importance, Nell said, 'Why, I do confess, this is a man beneath me, of that I'm sure. The worm stirs. Mmm. It stirs indeed – and what a worm. Er, gentle audience, what size are the worms in this part of the kingdom?'

She didn't wait for a reply, although several people said the largest in the country, even giving size, for she continued: 'I feel . . . I am sure . . . It is very much a man I'm on. I feel the point of the matter . . . and it is a man with much point . . . Pray, sir, are you a man of point? And, if so, do you know it is rude to point?'

Each of Nell's calculated pauses brought laughter, and she turned now to Rochester, who was enjoying her show: 'Do you know, m'lord, that your cousin has point? Very much point, I must, hesitatingly, add. Yet is it not a fact that there has never been much point to your family? But what point is this? I must, verily, investigate it. Perhaps, alas, I only imagine it to be point.'

She began to search with her hands and Rochester, seeing that Strang was crimson with embarrassment, ended the jest. He said, loudly, 'The point, my child, is it is long past your bed-time. Landlord. Hustle the would-be-hussy to a virtuous couch for the night, lock her in, and keep safe the key.'

Before Nell could continue the monologue, the huge landlord swooped, lifted Nell, wriggling and screaming from Strang's lap, folded her naked limbs in the protection of the cloak she had abandoned, and carried her towards the stairs, followed by laughter. Nell kicked and screamed, but it was of little use.

The landlord made the mistake of pausing at the staircase, so that Nell, in a sense, could take a bow to the storm of applause. It enabled Nell to clear her young lungs, and yell, 'If you will find me, my Lord Rochester on the night of my fifteenth year, look for me in Sir Harry's bed.'

She tried to say more but it was lost in the cheering and the applause, in which Rochester led.

The two wenches joined Rochester's table, and the blonde tucked herself into Nell's vacated seat. Roberts and the two other men went into the yard, from whence there came a fearful noise. Rochester explained that the bear was being put on his mettle by having live cats tossed to him before the dogs were let loose.

There was food and wine in plenty yet, and Strang was already intoxicated; and noise or not from the yard outside, he knew that on this night he wouldn't get much sleep. People served themselves better near the towns than in the country, he observed, and all a man needed was the will and a shilling.

Chapter Seven

He was the most feared man in London, yet very few knew him either by sight or by name. All they knew was that he was there, somewhere, and not too far from the King and his Government. He had one of the largest rooms near the palace. but one which was tucked away to the rear, away from the drawing rooms and the gardens, the fashionable and from the frivolities. Even King Charles, it was said, shuddered when his name was mentioned. But Charles was a kind-hearted man, a man who wanted to love his neighbour – especially his neighbour's wife, it was said.

His name was Redeeming Hawkins, Redeeming because his parents had been religious, and with his periwig awry and his clothes crushed, Strang was reminded of a faded schoolmaster who had spent too much time and had dried out in a classroom. Master Hawkins had eyes which were everywhere because he had spies everywhere. He supplied evidence to the Star Chamber, to the King, to the criminal courts and to the Church. He ensured that people were not only living in the way prescribed by law, but praying in the manner called for by the established Church.

Even the Earl of Rochester was nervous when they were shown into the long room, with its shelves packed with boxes and parcels of papers. Every one would be a document, Strang reflected, and perhaps they went right back in history to the Tudors and gave evidence against traitors and religious martyrs long since burnt, beheaded or hung, drawn and quartered.

Master Hawkins had a pleasant manner and was respectful of nobility even though, as Rochester later nervously gloated, 'I bet the rum-rascal has a lengthy file on my misdeeds.'

'Good day, my lord,' he said. 'And to you, Sir Harry,' he added after Rochester introduced them. He made polite conversation at first. 'His Majesty looks fit, don't you think?' and 'Fine weather for the season of the year,' and 'Did you see

Master Drake's execution? I hear he died well. The devil led me a fine dance, I tell you, before I nailed him right.'

Rochester mentioned the matter to hand. He began, defensively, 'I'm not sure, mind you, Master Hawkins, if the matter be important or not.'

'All matters are important, my lord. Many step close to the edge of the law by perverse design or by accident, m'lords. A slight shift in law, which happens, can make a patriot a traitor, a Christian a heretic. We do live in troubled times, but I think all times are troubled. Man thrives on trouble. It is a canker in his nature. He needs it so much, I do believe, that he rushes towards it. And if it wasn't religious conflict, it might be something more dangerous . . . treason?' He blinked as if he had uttered a vile oath.

Rochester said, 'You confirm my own opinion that religious controversy is a red herring, deliberately so.'

'Then, my lord, take this from one who wishes you well, your thoughts are dangerous. Do, I beseech thee, purge them. But, as I say, don't be nervous about bringing me bad news. As I say, I thrive on it. It gives me gainful employment, and if it didn't, I doubt not that I'd be mixed in mischief too.'

They had discussed the matter all morning after hearing Nell's full account of Fox's affairs. Rochester, believing Fox dangerous, decided the authorities must be told. Strang, although reluctantly, had come to the Spymaster, Redeeming Hawkins, with him.

Rochester told the story, surely a commonplace one, with brevity and skilful clarity, of how religious lunatics had spirited a girl away from the loving care of a harlot mother. Before he reached the end, he interjected, 'What is strange is the fierce battle these zealots put up before they would yield her. But for the determination of our attack, and courage, we would have lost the day and the girl.'

Agreeing that it was unusual for Quakers to fight, Hawkins volunteered the information, unnecessarily, Strang thought, that he dealt only in matters pertaining to the security of the State. 'You have told your tale with great skill, my lord,' he added, 'but it can only appeal to the romantic, and not the professional, in me. To give definition, my lord. You may say, as you might already have said, that the King is deficient in bed. It would be unwise but not treason to say it. However, if you say the King is deficient as a Sovereign, then you sail in troubled waters and interest me.'

Rochester said hotly, 'I apologise for telling my story badly, sir. I also thank you for the lecture. But I hadn't yet come to the point.'

Hawkins bowed and smarmed his apologies.

'The leader of this scurrilous pack is a lunatic,' said Rochester.

As if switching sides and showing anxiety to please, Hawkins replied, 'My Lord, if he is a lunatic I am interested. They give us vexious troubles, lunatics. They rush to us for racking and hanging.' His eyes narrowed. 'What did he do to the girl? Did he swive her?'

'No, he thrashed her, sir. For her many sins – or so he said.'

Hawkins smiled. 'They always find excuses, that they do.'

Rochester, hiding his distaste, continued, 'it is what this child overheard during her captivity . . .'

'In between her chastisements?' Hawkins volunteered.

'That,' added Rochester, 'made me think it was a matter for you. He talked wildly against the state and against the King. He said the sinful of London would be cut down by an invisible disease, and he talked about a great day of reckoning which would come on an east wind bringing death and destruction by burning to the Babylon, as he called it, which was London.'

Hawkins lifted one point from the speech and played it lightly on his tongue. 'An east wind bringing death and destruction by burning? Mmm. This interests me, my Lord, for I don't recall that as a quotation from the Bible, do you?'

Rochester said pompously that the Bible was the only book he was not on familiar terms with, and Hawkins licked his lips and smirked mischievously at him. 'I remember what I would say when we had a war against the Catholics, my Lord. I would look at a man directly and snap, "Are you a good Catholic." He would, usually, say either Yes or No, but, of course, you see, both answers are wrong. The reply should be "I am not a Catholic".'

Rochester studied the table with silence, Hawkins coloured, and then continued. 'The point, my Lord, is that these religious lunatics, of which there are now many varieties – another sign we live in uncertain times – gabble outlandish nonsense like this all the time. It is usually something stolen from the Bible about the wrath to come. However, when they have the ingenuity to invent calamities of their own I become, at one and the same time, intrigued and troubled. If they can invent the idea, they may well have the dexterity to put it into physical practice, if only to prove that their prophesy be right.'

The same idea had been discussed by Strang and Rochester but not at such a fine and learned point. Hawkins, although objectionable, had a shrewd twist of mind and Strang would hate him as an opponent. He was to be told that Hawkins was always in the dungeons when a suspect was put to the Question, and the vision of it had sent a shiver through his blood.

'But nobody has yet mentioned the name of this wretch?'

'Preacher Fox,' said Rochester. 'A Fighting Quaker.'

'We know him well,' said Redeeming Hawkins, 'but we thought we had unburdened him in the direction of America.'

Something told Strang that Hawkins was lying and that he had never heard of Fox at all; but to save face and office, he pretended he had. Later Rochester would confirm that he also felt that Hawkins had never heard of Fox before their arrival.

'Is he dangerous?' Rochester asked.

Hawkins didn't answer the question, but seemed to wish to change the subject. He turned suddenly on Strang. 'You are the silent one, Sir Harry, pray what do you think?'

'If it is of interest and value, sir,' Strang replied, 'I think Fox deserves watching, but I don't think he should be persecuted because his ideas are out of joint with those of the times or are colourful.'

Hawkins betrayed nothing in the smile he gave Strang. After a pause, he said, 'With King Charles as monarch, he won't be persecuted for his ideas or his religion. But these men, Sir Harry, are insane to a point of much danger for us all.'

Rochester had been subdued and a little overawed by being in the presence of the Spymaster. But now, suddenly, his manner changed and he was the flippant courtier again.

'Which suits you well, sir, since it keeps you busy and yourself out of mischief.'

Hawkins didn't take offence. He said, 'I didn't know that Fox had returned from New England. Nor that he and his followers now went about heavily armed. Nor, for that matter, did I know he had developed a taste for girls, even if it was only for spanking them. For all this information I am indeed in both your debts.'

Rochester still played. 'Which is better than the reverse. If we were in debt to you, Master Hawkins, I would think it a racking matter.'

Strang tried to warn Rochester with a lift of his eyes. The

very devil was in his cousin now, but Hawkins, with a disarming smile, replied, 'Your cousin, Sir Harry, thinks I have the tolerance of a King.'

'Any man who is worthy of his manhood can afford tolerance, sir,' said Rochester calmly. 'Pray, sir, how many shoulder-blades have we broken today?'

'I fear my Lord of Rochester is bored, Sir Harry, and would away to wine and women.'

'Both pursuits, sir, which I respect by giving them good attention. What peculiar antics do you involve yourself in, may I ask, to get a prick-rise?'

'Since your kinsman is out of sorts, Sir Harry, a question or two to you?'

'Of course.'

'I would value your opinion, Sir Harry, since I respect it, on your estimation of Preacher Fox as a man.'

'I cannot give you that,' said Strang, 'for neither my cousin nor I have come face to face with him.'

'He might have developed an insane fixation for this unhappy child and again attempt to take her from this harlot.'

'A faithful servant watches the house,' Rochester said sourly.

Hawkins didn't press them for the girl's name and address, and neither of them intended to tell him. 'I suppose, Sir Harry, the varmint excused the kidnapping on the grounds that he was rescuing the child from a whorehouse?'

'A whore's house,' Rochester corrected smoothly. 'The child has but one mother.'

Hawkins talked as if he were thinking aloud. 'I'm not interested in minor errors. But they can be useful to put away a man if you can't hold more serious matters against him.'

'What is this, sir?' Rochester sneered. 'A traitor-taker without a taste for torture! The rack, sir; rack him, you neglect your work.'

'One, my Lord, never gets the truth one wants when one racks a suspect. The victim too readily confesses to you that which he thinks you want to know. This is no truth at all. I do like to know the truth. I am a great one for the truth, my Lord.'

'So?' said Rochester. 'Innocent or guilty, to the rack with him.'

Hawkins smiled at Strang as if sharing a joke with him about Rochester, and he said, 'In man's eyes all are guilty, my

Lord. In God's eyes only are all innocent. Nobody is innocent. All are guilty . . .'

'If all are guilty then all are innocent, Master Hawkins, for both words become meaningless.'

'Now we will beat the bush about logic,' Hawkins said with a sigh. 'I fear, Sir Harry, I must saddle you with your kinsman, and hurry you hence from here.'

Strang was pleased to be going. He felt uneasy in the Spymaster's presence. Hawkins walked them to the door. Away from his huge desk, his incriminating papers, his bells for ringing brutes, much of the menace seemed to leave Hawkins and he became, in complete contrast, a slug-like, mincing toady, who smirked at them as he dry-washed his hands.

'It is presumptious of me to so say it, Sir Harry,' he said, as he opened the door for them; 'but you show a trust in people and a kindness which is rarely seen in London. I say to you, sir, with all respect, be on your guard.'

Rochester was already moving for the dark staircase after only lifting his hand in a perfunctory gesture of farewell; and Strang, hurrying, caught him up.

There was a sharpness in Hawkins's voice as he uttered his parting words. 'Pray, gentlemen, do watch your step.'

Even though Strang felt that the Spymaster was referring to the staircase, which was dark, and not their personal activities, he felt numbly chilled as he descended the stairs.

Chapter Eight

IN the space of as many minutes Sir Harry Strang spent as many pounds as the Earl of Rochester dragged him from one shop to the next in the Strand arcades. With but a hundred pounds between him and penury, barely enough to keep him living with the appearances of a gentleman, for a twelve-month, his cousin was easily telling him to spend it all.

Rochester became impatient and angry at one stage, and reminded him that a gentleman was known by the expense he put on his back not by his wit or his bravery. 'If you present yourself at the King's court as a poor man,' Rochester warned; 'I'll swear no knowledge of you nor admit a family connection.'

He added that Strang should follow the example of himself and Buckingham who had set the precedent of rarely, if ever, paying their tailor bills. 'The shopkeepers welcome us because we set the new French fashion, and we advertise their cloaks by wearing them.'

'That might be fair for you and my Grace of Buckingham, but I am but a country baronet, not an earl or a duke,' Strang shrewdly observed.

They became so heated in the shops that they almost came to blows and caused much head shaking and shrugging among the shoppers. Time and again, Rochester insisted that Strang buy himself some gaudily coloured frippery, and each time Strang said he would rather be dead than have such girlish nonsense on his back. Ineffectively, Rochester argued for the importance of clothing, maintaining that if you removed the crown from a King, or the uniform from a general, you were left with just a man like any other man.

'I have a title, and I am a man. I hope, cousin, a better man than my title.'

Rochester had simmered down and had become reflective, but he was determined to win Strang over by soft and clever counsel.

'At court, where most are titled, titles have little importance, cousin,' Rochester counselled. 'But wit and intelligence help, especially if accompanied by flamboyancy and high spending. These attract. They always have, and they always will. It matters not to the King you are poor, and he – he has been poor himself – will do something about it when he can. But let not the Johnnies-lately-at-court know of your impoverishment. Spend heavily today in the anticipation of being rich tomorrow. And, in betwixt, the King and I will seek a wealthy bride for you.'

Strang rasped, 'I'll not marry for money, cousin.'

'Then,' snapped Rochester, 'I'll not keep you.' He relaxed immediately. 'What better reason for marrying than for money? Then you marry not only for your bed but for your board.'

'Why not follow your own counsel?' Strang retorted. He was scowling at the gilt sword, costing two pounds, which Rochester had made him buy for court wear. The terrible waste angered him.

Rochester, without anger, said, 'I am working on it. I will have Lady Elizabeth Malet and all her thousands before the year is out. I swear on it.'

Strang was sceptical. Rochester had been imprisoned in the Tower for kidnapping the heiress, and she would hardly have permitted this if she would have Rochester. But Rochester thought the mistake he had made after carrying her away was not attending to her ruin immediately.

'I do believe she secretly fancies me,' he said, 'and the committal to the Tower was done to give the affair notoriety. Meanwhile, I remind her constantly both that I am alive and clever by sending her poems.'

'I have no talent for poetry,' said Strang.

'You should try and gain it. It works wonders at a seduction, for any man may send a swain flowers. But, damn me, it is often hard work, and look at all the effort I would have saved had I swived Lady Elizabeth on the spot?'

After a rest, it was back to the shops again. A periwig cost Strang £3, and there was more expense on silk stockings, high buckled shoes, lace and silk cravats and ruffs. A plain plum-coloured shallon suit was selected for city wear, but the largest expense went on a golden suit of shot-silk for the court with necessary accessories which cost Strang a stupendous £13.

It made Strang feel no easier that he had signed for all the goods instead of paying cash, for he was neither the Earl of Rochester nor the Duke of Buckingham, and he would certainly pay the money when the call came.

Fortunately Rochester soon tired of ordering clothes that he would not himself wear, and sent an attendant for a reliable porter to carry the goods to Strang's lodgings in Fleet Street. When the man arrived, Rochester said, 'Harry, give the man a couple of coppers and bid him hurry hence.'

Strang did as he was told, and they went into the Strand, leaving the man with the parcels. Strang looked back nervously, and Rochester said, 'Worry not, Harry, the entire morning's work has cost you but two-pence.'

They turned right towards the Charing Cross and before they got there, they saw a crowd of noisy people gathering in the square. Beggers lined the curb as they approached, dirty and scab-covered, wearing filthy rags for clothing, and Strang was immediately reminded of the foul contrasts in the quality of life in the capital. There was a ruder shock awaiting him as they turned the square.

'Somebody is being pilloried,' Rochester said with quickening interest.

The pillory stood on a raised platform. It was of polished dark wood which made it look all the more evil and frightening. It looked like a man-sized letter 'T' stood upright, and there was a large round hole in the centre for the victim's neck, and two smaller holes on either side for his hands. The victim would be faced against the pole and his head and hands thrust through the circles, whereupon a bar would be brought down and he would be firmly locked in, head exposed to the crowd.

Rochester said with contemptuous superiority, 'I suppose he is the fruit of Redeeming Hawkins's labours.'

People were hurrying excitedly into the square, and Strang could sense the prickly tension among them. Here was sport for ready, willing hands. Tradesmen came too, and with an extra interest, lugging their wares, farm people with rotting vegetables and bad eggs, especially saved for pillory days. Bakers and custard-mongers were there with baskets of mushy pies and iron-hard bread.

Strang saw the victim. He was being lifted from a waggon and dragged forward. He looked a weak and sorrowful character, old and dried out, with a shining, perspiring face and damp, whispy grey hair on his balding pate.

People saw him and jeered, and that was ominous. Strang

had never seen this punishment carried out before but he knew that its severity depended upon the victim's popularity or lack of it with the crowd. If he was liked, nothing much would happen. It could be that he was so liked or sympathised with that nothing would be thrown at him and after spending the time prescribed by the magistrates in the frame – three or four hours – he would be allowed to leave. If he was neither popular nor unpopular the crowd would have sport with him by throwing eggs, stale food and bad vegetables and fruit at him, which often got out of hand as the bloodlust grew in them, and sometimes stones and bricks were thrown. If the man was hated, the pillory was as good as a death sentence, for the soft materials would be followed by bricks, stones and pieces of iron and in an hour the pinioned man could be battered to death with a fractured skull.

Rochester didn't know the man or his crime and crossed to some watchful officials to discover the matter. Strang saw him talking at great length to a man who carried a deputy sheriff's staff of office.

Rochester told Strang to expect the bloody worst on his return. The victim was a journalist named Gordon Thomas who had urged religious toleration in his writings and had been accused of defending the Pope, praising Catholicism, and deriding Anglicanism. Strang already noticed an unhealthy excitement among the crowd and the taunts they threw at the prisoner were heavily spiced with malice. Many had come with bulging pockets and carrying their own small bundles, and few were bothering to buy the stale bread, bad vegetables or over-ripe fruit from the vendors who nagged at them. 'I have loaves as hard as brickbacks reserved for the occasion,' said a salesman, approaching Rochester.

'Then stuff them up your arse, sir,' Rochester responded.

Now the victim was locked in the contraption. Only his head and hands were revealed to the crowd, and he had no room to move in. The public executioner stepped on to the platform carrying long-bladed scissors.

The crowd became excited, and Rochester observed, 'They're going to have his ears first.'

Strang noticed that even his cousin, who was against such brutal nonsense, could make a jest about it. 'Yonder Thomas looks less an ass without his ears, Harry,' he observed, with a nervous laugh.

The common executioner was swift and efficient which

seemed to add more to the cruelty and inhumanity of the occasion. Strang heard a hollow snipping sound as the man's left ear was removed. A cheer broke from the crowd. In a moment, the hangman was on the other side of the pillory, there was another snip, another cheer, and now he held up an ear in each hand for the audience to see that his work had been done. When, however, he stepped from the stage, there were hoots of complaint.

Voices in the crowd called derisively to the under sheriff and his officials, demanding to know why Thomas's nose hadn't been slit and which of them had taken bribes.

A man said crossly to Strang, 'We allow too much tolerance. Or corruption. It could mean our deaths.'

Rochester peered around Strang. 'Do me the pleasure of pissing off, sir,' he said amiably. The man, glaring at them, moved to some friends and began to complain darkly about Rochester and Strang. The disappointed crowd, however, now took his attention, for they began to pelt the victim, who already had blood running down his cheeks and looked curiously misshapen without his ears.

The air had become thick with missives, and the hangman, laughing, was running to get out of the way. One or two people deliberately let fly in his direction. But in the main the missiles smashed against Thomas, who could move hardly an inch to avoid them; though he held his head down to protect his eyes. Eggs spattered his face and body, to be followed by squashy pies and over-ripe fruit; but these, although they created the impression of violence, did him little harm. It was the material which was to come which would draw blood and break bone. In moments he was unrecognisable, a black, white, pink and red gooey mess covered him and spattered the platform and woodwork about him.

Some of the vendors, putting pleasure before profit, began to throw their stock at Thomas, but in the main they now hawked vigorously among the watchers, tempting those who had used up their ammunition. There was an indefinable tension now, and Strang became aware of it. It was as if the crowd were waiting for the real show to present itself. Strang turned to Rochester and said he wished it could be stopped; but Rochester, flintily, told him that it was impossible.

'You have fame and personality, cousin,' Strang persisted, 'you can laugh the mob out of this hateful mood.'

'You don't understand,' Rochester said miserably. 'Such a

business, even if the King tried it, would be fraught with peril. Already it is whispered that the King shows too much religious tolerance and that, secretly, he is a Papist. Look, let us be away from this misery. Thomas put himself there. I didn't. He is a fool. Let him, certainly, believe what he wishes to believe, but let him learn to be discreet with his pen and walk not too much out of step with the mood of the times.'

'The mood of the times is created by the leaders,' Strang argued. 'This mob is mindless. It is up to people like you to give them mind.'

Rochester scowled sourly and cynically, 'Perhaps we need events like this to keep the mind of the mob from real concerns.'

Rochester seemed to know what would come next and decided to take his cousin away. He took him by the arm and turned back from the crowd, saying, 'Don't attempt to understand the complexity of London and Londoners all in a day, Harry.'

Strang looked back once before they turned into the Strand. There was a terrible stillness about the crowd. Nothing, nobody moved; and Thomas just stood at his frame, his head down, waiting; and Strang, miserably, worried what his thoughts might be.

In a trice Rochester had shrugged the ghastly business off. He skipped over the cobbles in the Strand and said, brightly, 'Cousin, let's drink.'

Before they had gone a few yards a loud roar of hatred came from the Charing Cross square.

Chapter Nine

THERE was a traffic snarl-up up the Strand, where it linked with Fleet Street, which brought tempers to the boil, and fisticuffs between a waggoner and the driver of a Hackney coach. Strang watched the men batter each other until blood flowed, and remembered his own clash with Lord Talbot almost on the very same spot. He had left Rochester, for he felt not like drinking; and he wished to be alone to reflect and assess. Much had happened since he had arrived in London. Never a dull moment, he thought sourly. Londoners were pasty-faced and sharply-witted and talked too fast and hurried too quickly. Quite suddenly, as at the pillory, you found yourself embroiled in violence. But there was much that sparked the imagination and caught at the mind. There was much to do that was not dull. As if they expected to die tomorrow, Londoners lived to the hilt today. The women were lovely. Never had he seen so many glorious women gathered in one place before. He thought of the beauties at court, and his own fine clothes, and the lovely Quaker lass with the red hair. There were fine taverns and no man need eat, drink or sleep alone, but there was a savagery and a crudity everywhere which shocked Strang.

Mistress Nan Quick saw Strang as he entered The King's Arms, and left her husband to speak and flirt with him. And here, Strang reflected, was another beauty, a little riper and maturer than some, but nothing amiss for that. She saucily scolded him for missing his sleep the night before and wished to know if he had been trying the mettle of London. He told her he had spent the night at Rochester's lodgings, and she reminded him life was short and nights shouldn't be wasted with family. Her flirtatious mood seemed to annoy her husband, who held back, but watched them.

'You look a little hang-dog, Sir Harry,' she said eventually, 'why not sleep until supper. I will bring you hot milk to your chamber.'

Strang reflected that he might have Nan Quick's fires to stoke if he did so, and another problem, in the shape of her husband, might present itself. He avoided the suggestion without giving offencé.

He told her he would sit in the garden at the back of the taproom and sip a cool ale, and he found a seat just outside the door. It was a pleasant afternoon with a soft breeze. The long narrow garden went on for a distance and ended in an orchard and above the apple and plum trees, Strang could see the masts of the ships along the Thames. There was a smell of flowers and fruit and the merry call of birds, but Strang was not at peace with himself. His thoughts churned. He recalled every incident of the pillorying in Charing Cross. Was Thomas finished now? He had a vivid mental picture of the journalist crushed against the wooden cross, his face pulped, his skull fractured – and his only crime being that he had urged tolerance and brotherly good nature.

His thoughts moved back, and he remembered Redeeming Hawkins, and the memory made him shudder. God, what had they done? They had gone to the vicious Spymaster and betrayed a fellow man whose only crime was that his ideas were extreme and didn't suit their own.

Hawkins hadn't been efficient in hiding his own inefficiency, and Strang, like Rochester had been, was sure Hawkins hadn't known about Fox until they had called on him. In doing this, they might very well have done Fox great damage, even threatened his life. Yet Fox had done them no harm. Even if his taking of Nell Gwynne had been partly to hit at the mother, he at least by his own fanatical views could justify it – for he was removing her from the depravity of Drury Lane and the wickedness of the theatre.

In betraying Fox he and Rochester had shown that same intolerance as the mob at Charing Cross who had stoned Thomas to death. It made Strang feel uncomfortable and dirty. He wondered if his cousin, Rochester, had the same worry at this moment, but perhaps not. His cousin was very strange and seemed to be fitted with a conscience which worked by fits and starts.

Beneath the sophistication and the cynicism, Strang knew Rochester to be a serious man who deeply wished that the world was a kinder place. Strang knew that Rochester, though he professed atheism, believed in a God, but could not visualise a God that permitted so much hatred and ugliness in the world.

Rochester, too, had a fine intellect, but because the world was littered by fools, he lacked the patience or the confidence, to try to change things. Much better to play and laugh, drink and wench and be popular as the court jester.

Rochester also saw religious controversy and persecution as a desirable thing, it seemed, as a red herring for the crowd to take their minds from more serious issues. Did Rochester reflect the mind of the King and his ministers here? Much better, say, to have the mob vent their sadism on harmless religious eccentrics than against the King and his Ministers.

Strang thought that such an attitude might appeal with the court since once already, and in living memory, a throne had been toppled and a King beheaded. Many people resented the King, and saw him but as an ordinary man. Rochester, for all his professed loyalty and love of the King, showed a certain ugliness and malice in his behaviour to both the King and his court. If there was much in life which offended Rochester's intellect, there was much about the frivolity at court which also irked him.

But Strang was sure of one thing now. He and Rochester had played Judas Iscariot. In a moment of intolerance, they had served Preacher Fox badly, and he might face the rack for their crime. It was a fact which must be faced and if possible, it must be rectified. Fox must be told, in some way. He must be warned. He must certainly be ordered to keep away from the Gwynne family, where his company was not wanted; and he must be alerted that the authorities might be interested in his extreme religious activities.

Strang's thoughts were interrupted by the arrival of two of the young wenches who seemed to be attached to the staff of the tavern. He nodded gravely to them and they seated themselves at a table close by, chatted and laughed, and tried to catch his eye. Strang assumed that Mistress Quick had sent them, thinking he had been too long alone. He wasn't in the mood for idle chatter but, with his eye to the future, he didn't want to give them offence or make them think he was a surly fellow, so he decided to go for a walk before supper. He caught up his hat, bowed to them in a courtly fashion, as he had seen Rochester do, and left the garden. Their giggles followed him into the street.

He turned in the direction, down hill, of Lud Gate. The street was abustle. Thunder was created by the iron-clad wheels of the heavy coaches as they rolled across the cobbles. The gate at Lud Gate, into the walled city, was narrow, and there was a traffic jam there, more yelling and cursing, and the threat of more violence.

This was Strang's first view of the ancient walled city and he stood looking at the now crumbling walls which rose some thirtyfive feet above him. Warfare had advanced a pace since they had been constructed and artillery and speed as devised by Cromwell for his New Model Army, would mean that walls would probably never give much protection again. It was as he approached the gate, that Strang's attention was caught by some oddities pinioned to the gate. His first reaction was that they were bits of dead dog or cat, but then he realised they were too large. They looked like pieces of wax, no longer shiny but covered by the grit and soot from the houses and street, and then realisation came and Strang felt sick. They were arms and legs to which tattered pieces of cloth still clung and on several the skin had been eaten away by birds and rats and the bone showed whitely through. Strang realised that they were what little remained of several people who had been executed and dismembered for high treason. He turned swiftly and hurried away, but the imagined stench of the relics didn't leave his nostrils until he reached Holborn, and the sweeter air which came from the fields on the north side of the road.

Strang was admiring some snuff boxes in a shop at High Holborn. He was in a better mood and amused himself by thinking that it was fortunate Rochester was not with him otherwise he would nag him to buy a dozen – and then he saw a familiar face. Seeing her again hit him with a jolt, partly because it reminded him of the near violence of their earlier encounter and partly because he saw again how lovely she was. Lovely women he had seen in plenty since his arrival, but there was something about this girl, in both her looks and carriage, which made her supreme above all the rest. She was dancing innocence and beauty combined. She was sweet, gentle, kind, modest. And all these virtues showed in her as she walked. But there was something else, something which he saw when her light blue eyes saw him, a candour and frankness, despite the innocence, which hinted at much.

She was the Quakeress, the beautiful red-headed girl, who had stepped in front of her father near St Dunstan's Church in the Strand the day before when Rochester had quarrelled with her father.

Strang acted on impulse. He had no plan, and he didn't know

what he would say and because of her puritan upbringing, he knew he would be rebuffed, but he turned and swept off his hat, showing that old desperation which had shown itself in the country, where attractive girls were scarce and he had used all manners of excuse, when he met one, to start a conversation. She would have passed him as he bowed without acknowledgement, when she hesitated, then stopped.

By now Strang had found something to say. 'Ma'am, a few words with you, if I may. I would apologise for the behaviour of my kinsman, the Earl of Rochester, yesterday.'

She had remembered him, for she replied immediately. 'Apologies, perhaps, should best come from John Wilmot himself. Certainly they are strange coming from you, for you owe us no apologies. On the contrary, my father and I are indebted to you and you should receive our thanks.'

Strang lied, 'But my cousin is most contrite. He has rebuked himself on the matter these past twentyfour hours, but he knows not how to make remedy in this matter.'

'John Wilmot, sir, has much that is amiss in his behaviour and it would surprise my father to hear that he knows not how to make amends. He knows my family by name and it would not be difficult for him to discover, if he does not already know it, where we dwell.'

This surprised Strang, and embarrassed him. He had been caught out. Rochester knew the family and an old malice seemed to have done as much as anything else to bring about the friction in the Strand. She saw his embarrassment however and laughter touched her lips and eyes and transformed her into such a radiant beauty, that Strang felt both weak and speechless. He managed to find words, eventually, and said, 'I do feel a duty, ma'am, to apologise on behalf of the family before my cousin acts on the matter.'

'But, sir, we have established that there is nothing for you to apologise for. You have served both your own family and my family well in this matter.'

She saw that the point had rendered Strang momentarily speechless and she smiled softly, and hurried to assist him. 'On reflection, sir, I believe my father would wish to thank you personally, for on his recovering from the ugliness of the situation, he said that we owed you much.'

'Not much,' Strang said hurriedly, 'my cousin has faults, but he would never have used the sword, I assure you.'

She shrugged. 'So, sir, I would suggest, if you wish it, that you call on my father. Evenings at about five of the clock are the best times.'

Strang bowed. 'Thank you, I will be honoured, ma'am, to call. My name is Strang,' he said, and recalling that Quakers objected to titles, he added 'Harry Strang.'

'Mr father is Master Heaven Templegate and I am Mistress Comfort Templegate.' She nodded on this and went to walk on, but Strang, saying that family business might take him from London shortly, wondered if he might visit the Templegates this very afternoon. She nodded agreement to this.

Did he imagine it? Was that pleasure which showed itself in her lovely eyes when he suggested a call so soon? He believed it was and after giving him the address, and wishing him a grave farewell, she passed on her way. Strang turned switfly back to look at the snuff boxes in the window. His body was tingling, his mind whirling. Secretly he looked to the left to watch her passing along the street. Her walk was enchantingly graceful, and she brought a brightness to the day.

He allowed her ample time to get lost in the crowd, then he followed at some distance, turned into Chancery Lane, and followed a sedan chair so that as she turned to go into her house, she wouldn't see him watching her. He got but a brief glimpse of her before she disappeared, but it was enough. He now knew the house and could make no mistake. It was already mid-afternoon and there was much to do. With a lightness in his step, Strang returned to his lodgings. He went straight to his chamber and unpacked his parcels. He would wear the plain city suit, he decided, with a plain cravat and lace shirt because, being Quakers, the Templegates would see any extravagent display as vulgar.

He attended to his toilet and his dress, with a vision of Mistress Comfort's loveliness always before him. Her severity of dress added, rather than detracted, from her beauty. Everything was perfect. Her walk, her talk, her smile, her seriousness in important matters. Would that he had Rochester's talent so he could compose a poem to her!

He knew he had at last seen the girl who, without any doubts or qualifications, he would want as his wife. There would be problems of course, problems raised more by her family than his own. Rochester would have him marry a heiress – and a Protestant one at that – from a titled family, if possible. But Strang was his own master. No doubt Heaven Templegate would raise objections when he discovered that Strang had a title and because he was allied to Rochester; but in the first flush of being in love, Strang swept all these fears aside. Instead his thoughts dwelt upon Comfort, striving to remember all that they had talked about, and the way she had looked at him, imagining meanings in everything she said.

He was too early when he left his lodgings for the visit. He was forced to kill time by pacing the length of Fleet Street several times before he eventually turned into Chancery Lane. Even so he was five minutes early when he hammered the front door of the house and was admitted by a smiling woman attendant. He was surprised that she didn't ask him his name before leading him through a room to the garden at the rear.

Strang saw upwards of a dozen people standing on the lawn halfway down the garden and Mistress Comfort was addressing them. They were in the plain habit of Quakers with the solemn expressions that he had learned to associate with these people. He stood on the path undecided and then, seeing him, Mistress Comfort came, with a smile, to greet him.

'I'm afraid my parent has been delayed abroad, sir,' she said, 'I do humbly apologise, and also for neglecting you awhile. I must attend to these good people.' She indicated a bench where he could sit, and then returned to the group.

Strang could not hear what she said at this distance, but he judged it to be some form of religious service for the people, of both sexes, soon formed a ring. They were not close enough together that they could touch so it was no round the pole May Pole celebration or anything frivolous in the same form. All of a sudden the people began to slowly clap their hands, and Mistress Comfort, in the centre, clapped in unison.

After the clapping stopped, the people began to shake. They rolled their heads from side to side and swayed their shoulders. Eventually the tempo became faster and they were also gyrating their hips. What Strang found peculiar about the dance, if dance it was, was that the participants never moved their feet btu stayed on one spot while they were in motion. Most of them had their eyes closed and seemed to be tranquil and at peace. Shortly Comfort Templegate joined him on the bench, and she, smiling, explained: 'It is my father's idea. He brought it from the Netherlands. It has earned the sect here, of which my father is the leader, the name of The Shaking Quakers.' She further explained, 'Our belief is that God is inside every one and you communicate with him by dancing.'

Strang, after only a moment's reflection, found commendation for it. 'It makes a change from receiving spiritual guidance by pompous lecture.' He hoped that she wouldn't discuss religion, however, because it was a subject he knew little about and, since he couldn't discuss it, she might assume him to be unlettered and stupid. He knew that Rochester, in this situation, wouldn't be at a loss for words.

She had reason now for the absence of her father, 'A disciple is near to death,' she explained, 'and my father is with him until the new beginning to share his joy.'

Strang revealed his astonishment, and she, laughing, explained:

'We, in our sect, think nothing of life on earth. It is but a purgatory of suffering to prepare us for the glories in the next. We see release, therefore, as joy.'

Strang watched her as she spoke, more captivated by the way she said things than by what she had to say. Anybody who thought life on earth was purgatory only had to look at her, for her beauty, he decided, showed up the lie. Life with Comfort would be a heaven on earth, but he dare not say it yet. 'You are a surprise to me,' he said, in answering her question on whether the sect astonished him, 'but only because I am a country bumpkin newly arrived in London.'

'We are a strict sect,' she said, 'and only a few have the conviction and the will-power to follow our laws. Abstinence, Master Strang, in all things is a virtue.'

Strang readily agreed that it was. He watched the dancers and wondered if he should join them, but thought it might look premature on his part. He was anxious to impress Comfort, and he guessed now that the Templegates had these services each afternoon at about five, so he could call again and profess an interest in the religion.

'When you meet my father,' Comfort said, 'you must not think he means any disrespect if he refers to King Charles simply as Charles Stuart, as he did your cousin, Rochester, by calling him John Wilmot. We believe, sir, that all men are equal and titles are meaningless.'

'I must confess,' said Strang, 'that I have a title myself. Only a small one. But I hate to use it since I didn't earn it. I am a baronet, a fortune or misfortune of birth, whichever way you see it.'

She laughed at this, but kindly so, and said, 'I think you think us very strange.'

Strang blushed. He did, but he wouldn't say it. He broadened out the conversation because he had remembered the Fighting Quakers and Master Fox. 'There are other non-conformist sects in London, I believe, Mistress Templegate?'

She agreed there was, and he asked if she had ever heard of one led by Master James Fox.

'I have indeed,' she said. 'He was friendly, once, with my father, and I too have met him. He is not, in our view, a true Christian, since he would change people by violence and not gentle persuasion. He heads a sect called the Sword of Vengeance. I can say no more because I am taught to say only the good of people and if I can't say that I must say nothing.'

'I would like to meet Master Fox,' said Strang, 'because I think I have it in my power to do him some service. Where might I find him?'

She hesitated before replying and Strang, remembering the man in the pillory, added, 'It is in my power to pass on to Master Fox a warning which might very well make him temper his behaviour with caution.'

She told him that Fox preached on Sundays in Moorfields but that she thought he could be found at other times in lodgings close by Shoreditch Church, which was just outside the Bishops Gate of the city.

After reaching a peak, the dancing slowed and at about six, the meeting broke up. When the congregation began to thank Comfort and leave, Strang felt that he should leave also.

She held him with her eyes. 'When next you call, sir, my father should be here to thank you.'

'I enjoyed both the service and your company, ma'am, and I would like to make it soon.'

A momentary doubt – or had he imagined it? – darkened her eyes, then was gone, and she smiled, telling him that the door was always open at five of the afternoon. Strang's exhilaration and joy stayed with him like a warm cloak on the way back to his lodgings. Nan Quick told him that Rochester with one or two noisy companions had called to see him, but had gone away again, but Strang seemed not to hear her, which made Nan Quick surprised. She watched him as he sailed into the garden and sent a girl with ale. Strang sat in the garden long after night had fallen, reliving every moment of the hour in the Chancery Lane garden.

Eventually the noisy sounds of supper being laid and the aroma of the food sent him scurrying into the eating hall where a knife, spoon and platter, and a jug of wine were ready for him. Strang wolfed the food and guzzled the wine, eating alone, his thoughts still on Comfort Templegate; but the reliving of the incident became brighter and episodes in which he danced alone with Comfort became more vivid as, unsuspectingly, he became drunker.

Often his thoughts about her became downright carnal and he was all on heat and it took a great amount of will-power before he could purify these thoughts. There would be none of that, he decided, until after they were churched. He wouldn't even demand that she lay with him, as was the custom, after the marriage contracts had been exchanged. However, the more he ate and drank, the more impure his thoughts became – and soon Nan Quick had joined him, scolding him for not doing justice to the platters of meat, poultry and vegetables before him. She was against his eating alone – which she thought bad for digestion and for the mind – and she sent the most docile of her young ladies to join him. Strang found it difficult to make conversation, so he drank the more. Eventually he knew he was more drunk than he had ever been, and he felt giddy and sick, and hurried into the garden. He reached the orchard down by the river before collapsing, and a long time seemed to have passed before somebody stirred beside him. 'No,' she answered, 'I'm not Comfort. I'm Nan Quick by name – and quick by nature.' She told him to be quiet and she took him in her arms, and Strang, believing her to be Comfort, became crazily alive.

Mistress Quick was delighted with his ardour and his energy, 'What care I,' she whispered, 'if you confuse me with another, as long as I get her benefit.'

Strang touched her lips to still them, hearing only Comfort's honeyed voice, and he closed his eyes as he worked so he could, the better, imagine her.

Chapter Ten

SIR HARRY STRANG left the tavern as soon as he could, and rode through Lud Gate into the city. Because the day was hot the lavender girls were out in strength, and Strang brought a twig of flowers to hold beneath his nose to stave off the stink in the narrow streets of the old city. He had left hurriedly because he wanted to forget Nan Quick and his misconduct of the night. If he could forget it completely, he attempted to convince himself, then he would not betray his guilt for what he had done when next he met Comfort Templegate. From this moment on, he would keep himself chaste for Comfort.

There was heavy traffic in the city, but eventually Strang left it through the Bishops Gate, and took the wide road with sumptuous houses on either side of it, which would bring him to Shoreditch. Gentlemen of business were coming into the city from their country villas and hawkers from the farms with baskets of fresh produce.

A group of laughing girls with carriers blocked his way at one stage and a girl called cheekily, "Sir, would you buy fine cabbages?" Strang said no, but said it with a smile, and the girl said she would be sold out by noon and would wait for him by the Bishops Gate. Strang remembered Comfort Templegate, killed his smile, then cantered on.

Soon he was at Shoreditch Church and by crossroads. To the right, the sign said *Hackney Village,* and because the cottages in the fields lay thick that way, he put his horse along the road by Shoreditch Church. When he reached the first cottage, he hammered on the door by bending from his saddle. An old country woman in a shawl – that by her looks could equally have been a man – answered his knock and contrived to appear both frightened and servile, aggressive and hostile by turn.

'I seek a Master James Fox,' he said.

She repeated the name twice, watching him as she did so, giving him the impression that she didn't like what she saw.

Eventually she pointed to a large wooden building enclosed by a yard further along the road.

Having pointed the way, she disappeared, slamming the door, and Strang was reminded once more of the hostility that people around London – possibly with good cause – showed to strangers. Still the sweet air of the country had put him in fine mood and he had only to look back to the walled city in the distance, and the smoke pall that seemed to hang like a halo above the spires of the many churches, to be reminded of cramped quarters and blotchy smells.

He climbed from his horse and led it at a leisurely walk to the building which he now saw was a blacksmith's forge. Through the open door and the dark shadows inside, he saw the rich red blast of flames of the fire, and in the reflection the sweat-glistening muscular arms of the smithie, who was hammering at a piece of glowing iron. Strang tethered his horse at a bolt and walked into the shed and the man turned.

Strang's attention was immediately attracted to the length of the hot metal. If this was about to be beaten into a horse shoe, the animal was of enormous size, for the metal seemed to be all of fifty inches in length. But now Strang saw a stack of long blades cooling against a wall and realised they were sword blades. The phrase, *the Sword of Vengeance,* crossed his mind, with Comfort Templegate sounding the words. He thought here was an enterprising smithie who, in betwixt waiting for horses to be shod, produced sword blades for sale. The bare-chested man spoke first. 'If you want a nag shoed,' he said in a matter of fact voice, 'you must wait for the smithie. Or take it elsewhere.'

The accent was country. There was authority, but not arrogance, in his manner. He wasn't exactly insolent, Strang decided, but just disinterested and detached. The man had a presence and perhaps too much character to show insolence. He was a country lad from ordinary country folk, Strang decided, and immediately guessed where he had got his bearing from. He would be an old soldier, and possibly an ex-officer of the Cromwellian Army, rather than the Cavalier.

As he approached the man, Strang decided definitely Cromwellian. The man respected Strang but only as an equal and, having said his piece, he waited for Strang to speak, before turning back to his work. Although he must have realised that Strang was a gentleman, he would not show subservience. Strang thought he would be in his mid-thirties, and this together with his manner of holding himself, made Strang more than certain that he was looking at one of the heroes of Oliver Cromwell's New Model Army.

'I'm not looking for the blacksmith,' said Strang. 'I'm looking for Master James Fox.'

The man lowered his hammer and stepped towards Strang, as if to get a better look at him, and Strang now saw that the man had bright red hair, and the colouring – although this was rougher texture – reminded him of Comfort Templegate's hair. But where hers was red and touched with blond, this man's hair was darker, almost ginger, in colour.

The man studied Strang carefully, now with a marked insolence, and Strang became irritable, and said sharply, 'I said I am looking for Master Fox; can you direct me to him?'

'Preacher,' said the man softly. 'Preacher Fox. He's changed his name, you see. He doesn't like James. That's the name of Stuart kings.'

'If it's a name worthy of a king,' said Strang, 'then who is a common man to complain.'

'I thought you might say that,' said the man, with a smirk. 'And not even English kings, but Scottish kings at that.'

Strang decided it would be against his dignity to argue the merits of the monarchy with this man. 'Preacher Fox then, since it suits him better and fits his calling. Do you know him?'

'I like not your sarcasm.'

Strang looked surprised. 'Sarcasm, sir? I meant it not as sarcasm. I'm a tolerant fellow, let Master Fox call himself by that title he wishes.'

The man's eyes flashed hotly, and he said, 'You still mock me.'

Strang found himself becoming annoyed. What was with this London? You civilly asked a stranger for information and found yourself embroiled in a conflict which could soon lead to blows. 'Sir, you do misjudge me,' Strang said, trying to contain his temper. 'Why should not Master Fox call himself Preacher if that is his business, much as a King whose business is ruling should call himself a King.'

'I am a leveller,' said the man. 'I believe all men are equal in God's eyes and all property should be equalled. . .'

'Then you are welcome to half of what I have,' Strang interrupted. He thought he detected a great violence in the man and guessed he was of a nature that if he had a title himself would be fiercer against levellers than anybody Strang knew. For Strang didn't care a damn about his baronetcy. If it was useful at times, it could also be an embarrassment.

'You still mock me,' said the man, but his manner had changed. It was as if the anger had died within him and he was no longer interested in Strang. He made a move and Strang side-stepped as if expecting the man to launch himself in an attack. The man smiled softly at this, as if it had confirmed something he already suspected, and he walked past Strang and stood in the road. He looked in both directions, left towards Shoreditch Church and right, across the fields, to Hackney. Then he re-entered the forge. 'Why would you be seeking Master Fox?' he said casually.

'That doesn't concern you.'

'Then who are you?'

'That doesn't concern you either.'

'You have given me, cavalier, two good reasons why I refuse to help you.' He returned to his forge.

'If Master Fox is a friend of yours and you would do him a service, sir,' Strang said angrily, 'you would tell me where I can meet him.'

He studied Strang with insolence for a moment, implying that he failed to see how Strang could be of service to Fox, and Strang reflected that here was a man who would never use good manners because he thought the use of them signified a sense of inferiority.

'Well?' Strang said firmly.

'Preacher Fox does reside nearby, though I happen to know that he is away for the best part of today. He is visiting the cake makers of Islington. If you consider it worth your while, I should return here about six of the clock. If you wish it, I will take steps to tell him to meet you here.' He was studying Strang now with a bright intensity in his eyes.

Strang bowed without mockery, thanked him, and left. He was riding away when he remembered that it was his intention to call again on Mistress Comfort Templegate. This, seemingly, would take an hour and he wouldn't reach the forge until after seven. He was on the point of turning back to rectify the appointment, but the man's rudeness made him change his mind. Let the smithie and Master Fox wait upon him. Strang was disconcerted to find himself in a sweat. The redheaded man had undoubtedly unnerved him, and it made him angry. The strength of the man, the authority in his bearing, had been something of a shock and a surprise. After all, it was clear that the man's background was humble. No doubt he had been a village lad, perhaps even a smithie, who had received the call from Cromwell and become a trooper in the New Model Army. His experiences there, and Strang guessed he had been promoted on merit to officer's rank, had given him the confidence he now showed. It was Strang's first real meeting with a Leveller and a Republican and he saw now why Cromwell's Army had created so much fear and had been invincible. Several thousand men like the redheaded blacksmith facing one on the field would be formidable indeed.

Strang crossed by the crossroads by Shoreditch Church, following the sign post which said Clerkenwell Village. Eventually he saw the village just to his right and across the fields to his left, London. He rode on again until he reached high ground.

Here he sat his horse awhile, undecided, but half a mile away across the fields he could see High Holborn and, on a pace, the buildings at the entrance of Drury Lane. He thought of calling on Mistress Nell Gwynne but decided that he didn't possess the strength, after the night before, to fight her off, and he would need have some rest so that he was alert and fresh to face Mistress Comfort. He hoped that her father would be away again, which meant he would have easy excuse to call on the morrow. He spied an orchard by the road and soft downy grass and in a trice he had tethered his horse and was slumbering beneath the larger of the apple trees. Only once was he disturbed – and then by two passing milk maids. One called to him cheekily that he could have her lips for a penny, and more things for more, but Strang, with barely a smile in reply, turned on his side and returned to sleep.

But Heaven Templegate was at home when Strang arrived and Strang found himself alone with him on the garden bench while Comfort, looking more lovely than ever, conducted the dancers on the lawn. Strang apologised to Templegate for Rochester's behaviour, which the old man gladly accepted, and Strang received profuse thanks from the sect leader for diverting an ugly incident. Strang thereupon added that Rochester was only jesting – if crudely so– and the old man's life was never in question. Heaven Templegate accepted this gracefully, and waxed philosophical. 'Life was woe, awaiting for Heaven,' he maintained, 'and people do react to it in different ways.' He himself found comfort in the Bible, but others, like

Rochester, in the bottle. He added that a lasting joy is found in the Good Book, but only temporary relief in the wine glass. Strang conceded he had a point. While the old man rattled on, Strang watched Comfort. She was an apparition of beauty and grace and more than her drop-jawed congregation, managed to enjoy herself and find excuse to smile. Templegate was getting on his nerves, but Strang had expected that. After all, no rose was without a thorn. The old man, however, was good and kind and harmless.

As he watched the shaking reach towards a frenzy, it crossed Strang's mind that some of the people, judging by their expressions, might be getting a sexual pleasure from the dance, however he promptly dismissed the thought with shame, for Comfort was out there among them. He next wished that Heaven Templegate would take a turn on the lawn and allow Comfort to rest beside him, and guessed the old man might have gout or a gammy leg which stopped him.

'There is much I like about Charles Stuart,' said Templegate. 'He has a frankness of mind and a tolerance about religion which is ahead of the times. He is as honest as a King is permitted to be, but why, oh why, is he such a fornicator?'

Then the old serving woman arrived with a jug of buttermilk and Templegate asked Strang to join him. While they were sipping this Templegate mentioned Preacher Fox, after saying that his daughter had mentioned Strang's interest in Fox. He continued: "It is not my business why you asked about him, nor do I pry. Don't misunderstand me, sir, but may I speak frankly?'

'You may, sir.'

Templegate added that he spoke with great difficulty because he avoided talking about people unless he could find something good to say about them, but he was in Strang's debt and felt compelled to warn him. 'I judge men personally, sir, and not by street gossip, and I knew Master Fox as a time as my friend. Therefore, I must warn you that he is a desperate man, a man of violence, who is consumed by great impatience and hatred.'

'I have heard as much about him elsewhere,' said Strang.

The old man nodded sadly. 'Such a fine brain. You wouldn't think, sir, that the common people could throw up such a man, but we will not conjecture into scandal on how this might have happened. All I wish to say on the matter is that Fox will not let sleeping dogs lie, but is determined to fan up the old troubles and hatreds between the common people and the royalist government.'

There he stopped and Strang thanked him for the warning, and Templegate became sad because he had talked ill of another human being. 'I hope, sir, I didn't give you the wrong impression? I strive to love my fellow man, I assure you, and do not idle the hours away in pernicious gossip.'

The conversation seemed to have exhausted and depressed Heaven Templegate, and Strang wondered if he should go. The old man, it became clear, was troubled by the fact that his duty had forced him to speak ill of somebody. Strang, touched by this and the old man's guilt, hastened to reassure him that it was not true, that by telling him of what he knew about Fox, he had done, indirectly, a service to Fox, which he might learn by and by.

Templegate accepted this and said that Strang was again doing him a service, but he was soon brooding on the matter again, and said he would go to his prayers to ask forgiveness of God. Before he moved off, he told Strang: 'By all means stay awhile, sir, and have discourse with Mistress Comfort. My daughter already looks upon you as a man of integrity and a valued friend. With this I concur. You are a finely set up young man, and should you wish it, my home is always open to you.'

Strang flushed and thanked him. The news that Comfort had spoken highly of him, filled him with joy. He watched Comfort swaying and clapping her hands on the lawn and, of a sudden, as if the devil was jesting with him, he got a fully frontal vision of Mistress Quick as she and Strang had struggled in a sweaty passion beneath the apple trees by the Thames. He felt mortified, and his guilt deepened when he remembered, as he swived with Nan, that he had substituted Comfort for her in his mind's eye during the action. His guilt coloured his cheeks and it was at that very moment, the dancers safely on their journey as they skipped in a ring, that Comfort hurried across to give Strang greeting.

It made him stutter and colour the more and she must have gleaned something of his thoughts and the truth made the joy leave her face for a moment and a graveness replaced it. She was skilled enough and gentle enough to hide the fact that she had learned something of the truth, and her mood became friendly, if not as bright as it had been, as she folded to the bench beside him. But Strang – reflecting later – thought that her conversation became as markedly stilted as his own.

She helped herself to buttermilk and Strang thought she was doing it to avoid talking to him. He saw hidden menace in her next remarks, for she asked him if he had exchanged compliments with her father and received thanks, and this, Strang saw, as an implied implication on her part that he now had no reason to call again. She recalled, too, that Strang had told her family business might take him soon from London, and asked when this might be.

Clumsy in his replies, Strang said lawyers were delaying his departure unnecessarily. He thought he might repair himself in her eyes by talking about his younger brothers and sisters all of whom, since his parents were dead, he had as his responsibility. She seemed to be impressed with the care and concern he showed while discussing this problem. Then Strang asked her if she had any brothers and sisters and immediately got an impression, which made him blush again, of four or five replica Comfort Templegates dancing on the lawn.

'I had three brothers and four sisters,' she said, 'but all were called to Heaven early. I alone was left to care for my father.'

Most families, which were large, lost three or four children, but the Templegates seemed to have fared badly, and Strang said he was sorry to hear such news.

His sorrow amused the girl, who laughed, and said the family had considered it an honour that God had called for her brothers and sisters so soon, and Strang, thinking it beneficial if you could look on tragedy in that light, didn't pursue the matter. But it crossed his mind that perhaps Templegate's own brand of religion, that death was a joy, had been something he had devised and convinced himself was fact after losing so many children – attractive children if Comfort was a good example. Strang again found himself watching the dancers, who were reaching a frenzy in their shaking, and again it occurred to him that they might be – at least some of them – experiencing a sexual spasm, though once more he promptly dismissed the thought from his mind.

Comfort helped by asking, 'Did my father mention Master Fox?'

'He did,' Strang said eagerly, 'and warned me about him.' And, on a sudden suspicion, he added: 'Did you ever see a powerful built man of about thirty-five years with ginger hair ever in Master Fox's company.'

She looked at him, frowning, and said, 'Sir, the description you just gave fits Master Fox himself.'

'I see,' Strang said, after he had recovered, but neither of them spoke on the matter again.

The dancers had soon reached a point of exhaustion and, looking contented and not as sad as they had earlier, they now began to leave. Mistress Comfort went to the garden gate to bid them farewell, and Strang was made miserable by the fact that several of the younger men strived to hold Comfort in conversation. His own meeting with Comfort this day had lacked something, and he put the blame on the carnal thought he had experienced just as Comfort had dashed to him from the lawn. He must strive, he decided, to keep sexual thoughts from his mind when he was with Comfort. But he knew, with deepening despair, that he was trying to reach the impossible.

One man lingered longer than the rest and something he said made Comfort laugh. Strang felt jealousy and hatred for the man. Such a lovely girl must undoubtedly attract a wide number of suitors, and she might feel compelled, and her father might also advise her, to select a husband from among her own class and following. The Templegates were not the sort of people who would seek to improve their position by marrying in a higher class and, besides, they were declared opponents of the nobility. All these things saddened Strang while he waited. He decided that he must declare his interest as soon as possible. If need be, he must bcome a Shaking Quaker and step on the lawn and jingle with the rest of them. He must show genuine interest in the weird sect until such time as Comfort was under his influence and he could turn her to more conventional worship. Certainly he must not have carnal thoughts while at Chancery Lane and it crossed his mind that it might be advisable to exhaust himself with the aid of Nan Quick and some of her girls before he came to the meeting so sex was the farthest thing from his mind.

When the people had finally gone, Comfort turned and looked at him. Since she had left the gate open and Heaven Templegate was still at his praying, Strang took it as a signal that he should leave. But now he must make her aware of his deep affection for her. She must have guessed what was coming by the grim-set of his jaw as he walked towards her, for before he could declare himself, she had said quickly, 'Thank you for coming, Sir Harry.' He didn't like her mentioning his title, which seemed to be a barrier between them. But before he could again form his words, she added: 'I hope, Sir Harry, that we will always be friends – true friends. Just friends, sir,' and colouring slightly, she continued, 'For I believe we can be nothing more.'

Even though the words were spoken softly, in Comfort's sweet voice, they cut to Strang's heart like the blade of a knife. In reflecting, he could remember nothing of what followed, what he said, how he reacted. When he came to recover, he was mounted and riding down Chancery Lane, and a group of people seemed to be interested in him and talking about him, and he recognised them as Quakers who had cavorted on the lawn. He could guess at their conversation. Why should a cavalier interest himself in the Quaker movement? Why indeed, he thought bitterly, and felt like driving his horse among them to really quake the Quaker in them. But he began to feel better by the time he reached Holborn. Comfort only *believed* they could be nothing more. That didn't completely rule him out. She wasn't committed to anybody else. It was but the class difference and the religious differences. She was obviously under the sway of her father and his outrageous and narrow theological ideas. Strang began to feel better. He must have patience and he must, above all else, persevere. He must be correct in his manner and in his dress, modest in speech and appearance, and on the morrow he would be out on the lawn twitching and cavorting with the rest of them.

He reminded himself that even though he had been of some service to the Templegates, the first meeting couldn't have been reassuring for them. Rochester might have been drunker, but Strang was sure that he had been drunk at the time, and would have revealed it in his speech, appearance and walk. He felt better by the time he had stopped cantering for he had convinced himself that he was reading too much into Comfort's farewell remark. Modesty decreed that Comfort, at this stage, say no more.

He found himself near the Black Bear and wondered if he might find Rochester there and seek his opinion. He found a familiar face in the taproom, but it wasn't Rochester's. It was Cooper, the servant his kinsman had left to watch over the Gwynnes, and he looked as if he had been seated there several hours and was quite drunk. Strang pounced upon him and accused him of neglecting his duty, but Cooper had ready reply.

'M'lord, it isn't so,' he declared. 'Nell Gwynne left by post-coach today. She has gone to stay for a spell with relatives in Islington Village.'

Islington, Strang thought. He did not like the sound of that. He recalled that the man in the Shoreditch forge had told him that Master Fox was visiting Islington on this very same day. It must be coincidence, Strang decided, but he thought it merited further investigation.

He went immediately to Nell's mother in the house in Old Bone Yard where at this time of evening the whores waited on every step. Strang had to push his way forcibly through a line of out-stretching and tempting arms. It did nothing to improve his temper for there was much now which puzzled him. His main thought was why Rochester, if he cared so much for Nell's welfare, allowed her to be raised in the stews of Drury Lane. Mrs Smith was ready with a cool answer. 'I thought it would be healthier for her to spend a few days with the miller at Islington, who is my brother-in-law,' she told Strang.

'I think ma'am,' said the puzzled Strang, 'that you should have consulted with my Lord of Rochester first. I understand Fox has connections at Islington.'

'That is news to me, sir,' she said.

With her permission, Strang helped himself to some of her French brandy, and then he bluntly produced a question that had taken shape at the rear of his mind. 'Ma'am, perhaps you could tell me, in confidence, why my kinsman takes such a lively interest in Nell?'

She looked surprised by the question. 'But surely, Sir Harry, since you too are involved, you already know.'

'Damnit, ma'am, it seems I know nothing. How am I involved?'

'Well, sir, Nell is kin to you – either a half sister or half cousin.'

Strang was speechless and was forced to seat himself as Mrs Smith, talking in her quick and nervous manner, related a tale these fifteen years old of how she, a slip of a girl, had been courted by two cavaliers simultaneously. One was Sir John Wilmot, the other his kinsman, Sir Philip Strang. They had knowingly shared Eleanor Smith and it was a tidy arrangement since they were kinsmen and often in London at different times from the other. In the confusion which had come with the Civil War there had been much unscheduled coming and going with both these gallant gentlemen, she said, so she was unable to say with any degree of certainty whether Nell was

Wilmot's child or Strang's.

Strang listened, with the anger growing in him. It had been a day, it seemed, of nasty shocks, and Mrs Smith was weeping by the time she finished her account, so much so that Strang assured her that his anger was directed against Rochester, not her.

'But why be hostile with your cousin, sir?'

'Two reasons,' said Strang; 'he kept the news that Nell might be my half-sister from me, but I think his gravest misconduct is in permitting a member of our family to live in the stews of Drury Lane, instead of providing her a good home and schooling.' This made Strang the angrier as he reflected on it.

Mrs Smith was smiling now. 'My Lord of Rochester has his reasons for this, Sir Harry. He believes Drury Lane and all it contains to be one of the finest schools in the world.'

Strang snorted. 'My cousin's humour is quite twisted and black at times.'

'But she will be an actress or a whore, sir,' said Mrs Smith, 'for what other calling is there for a girl without an inheritance, and even if she had this she would be but a whore for a penniless husband?'

'I detect the Rochester authorship in that remark, ma'am, and I'll not argue with it.'

She attempted to comfort Strang. 'Nell has never come to harm and her character has developed a pace. She is chaste still.'

'Only just,' said Strang. He was remembering the night at Notting Hill Barnes and how Nell had attempted to seduce him. The recollection of it made him angry again for he had almost finished the night in bed with a girl who could be his half sister. Rochester should have warned him by telling him the truth, especially as he must have seen the way things were going between them. He remembered too that Rochester had declined to answer Nell's blandishments himself which, he had to concede, was a mark in his cousin's favour.

Strang sought more information, and Mrs Smith told him that she could not be certain who was Nell's father and she wouldn't hazard a guess – 'Although my Lord Rochester is quick to declare, because of Nell's wit, that she is his sister. He says, forgive me, Sir Harry, that the Strangs are too dull to have produced a Nell Gwynne.'

Strang snorted at this.

The years of the Civil War had been hard on her, said Mrs Smith, for she no longer received protection from Sir Philip Strang, who had been killed, and the first Earl of Rochester was in hiding on the Continent. She had been forced to put herself under the care of an ex-royalist soldier named Gwynne, but he had been so badly wounded that the only protection she received was his name, and necessity had forced her to turn her back on virtue and welcome sordid guests.

Touched by her story, Strang told her to cease weeping and that he would see that a pension was forthcoming from the Rochester and Strang estates.

'My Lord of Rochester,' she said, 'has already arranged a small allowance. Moreover, he has great plans for Nell, both as an actress and as a mistress of the King.'

'Dreaming is one thing, ma'am, actuality another.' Strang stopped. He remembered he had certain dreams of his own.

'But, Sir Harry, the King has met Nell and is much taken by her.'

Strang was forced to agree that Nell was exceptional and that her waggish humour and originality of character would appeal to almost anyone. Rochester was interested in the main chance and would be aiming high. If he could get Nell Gwynne accepted by Charles as a mistress, it would strengthen his own position at court. Moreover he would have an ally who had the King's ear in private.

Strang could see the possibilities. Good men had hazarded their own wives for as much. What was good for Rochester, was as good for him, and he had a momentary vision in which he saw himself, finely robed, at court, an Earl now like Rochester, and with Comfort Templegate as his Countess – for not even she could refuse an earl – attending on the King. Then there would be a bonus extra, for Comfort being virtuous would never succumb, like other wives, to the amorous advances of the king.

Strang toyed with the dream for a moment, then quickly brushed it aside. His immediate concern must be Nell Gwynne, who was either a sister or a cousin, and could be in some danger.

There was the puzzle at Shoreditch. The ginger-headed man had said Preacher Fox was at Islington. And now he discovered that Nell, once Fox's prisoner, was also at Islington. It was a coincidence he didn't like. Moreover, when he had described the man in the forge to Comfort Templegate, she had vouchsafed that his description fitted Fox. Had he been talking to Fox in the forge and not known it? Why should Fox pretend to be somebody else and then invite him to return in the evening to meet Fox?

He remembered that nobody would know Fox more than Mrs Smith, who had been his mistress, and he immediately asked her to describe the preacher. She did so and in height, age, and colouring, she described the man Strang had seen at the Shoreditch blacksmith's forge. She made particular mention of the bright lustre, which some people found frightening, in his eyes, and Strang knew that the man he had met could only be Fox.

He was already late for the appointment he had made, and it would be dark before he reached Shoreditch, but he knew he could not rest until he had investigated the puzzle further. Making his excuses to Mrs Smith, Strang left to ride to Shoreditch.

Chapter Eleven

THERE was no moon and no stars and the night was as black as King Hal's heart, thought Strang, recalling a phrase handed down by his Tudor grandparents. He cantered along the tree-lined lane known as Old Street, doubting his wisdom in travelling so late, for he hadn't even returned to his lodgings to collect his saddle pistols, and only had his rapier for his protection. The only illumination was provided by the seemingly linked ribbons of light from the houses of London, which were to his right. But eventually he saw the wider road which led from the Bishops Gate and knew, when he turned onto it, Shoreditch Church, the ancient 700-year-old pile, would be ahead of him. He thought meanwhile of Rochester, with anger, for if Nell Gwynne, who could be his sister, was still chaste, it was only just so, and he thought of Comfort Templegate with love, and hoped that he might not only bring about a reconciliation between Fox and Templegate but show himself worthy in the doing of it. He caught up with a post-coach with a link-boy galloping ahead, and immediately fell back to keep his distance, lest they took him for a highwayman.

He eventually saw the church and the coach lumbered on through the mud in the direction of Stoke Newington, and Strang found himself alone by the church, looking into the impenetrable darkness along the Hackney Road. He greeted the blackness with mixed feelings for it brought back old memories of his country home when he had set out, after a session of boredom, to find a bright inn, drink and wenches, and been hopelessly lost and had to retreat to his home with failure. London might have much about it which annoyed him, but it was a sure cure for boredom. Vaguely, against the horizon line, he identified the blacksmith shed, but no light came from it, but since he was almost two hours late for his appointment, he couldn't expect Master Fox to be waiting. He could try the building, however, and if this yielded nothing, then seek at a cottage or a tavern for Preacher Fox's whereabouts. He jogged towards the building, and it was as he was almost there, that the rogues made their attempt upon him. He saw the blazing faggot first, which they had shielded by the trees, and which was now held aloft by the nearest horseman as if he was attempting to identify Strang before they attacked him.

There were two of them, and they were both mounted, but the very fact that the robbers wished to identify their victim before they struck, which was unusual with highwaymen, worked to Strang's distinct advantage. For a start, he saw the flaming torch as the riders spurred from the trees. The man with the blazing branch held it high and forward, the better to see Strang, and yelling, 'It's him!' threw the torch to the road, presumably, to free his hand for a weapon. The other mounted man had taken aim with a pistol but the suddenness of their rush and the faggot soaring through the air, not only made Strang's horse spook, but brought it up high with its forelegs in the air. At this moment the man fired his pistol, but Strang, to keep his seat, was bending low around his horse's neck, and the ball went wide.

Strang knew that he was possibly better mounted than the men, even if he had come on a two-mile journey, and he responded by raking his horse's flanks with his spurs, and the mount, regaining the ground, bunched its muscles, and went forward at a leap.

But the second man was still coming at him, presumably to strike him with his empty pistol, and yet Strang couldn't reach him, nor had he time to draw his sword. But he could strike the man's horse, if not the man, and this he did, punching hard at the animal's head. His gloved fist hit squarely and had instant effect, for the animal sprang high in the air, and taken by surprise, the robber was unseated.

Then Strang was away, pounding through the darkness of the Hackney Road, and with nobody in pursuit of him. He kept up the pace for the best part of a mile until he came to crossroads. There were signposts but no light to read them and he had to wait some minutes before a coach, accompanied by link-boy riders, came into sight. He discovered that he was on the Cambridge Road and that if he turned right he would reach the Mile End Road and the city by the Ald Gate, and following the coach at a distance, he made his way back to Fleet Street in this manner.

Supper, which lasted two or three hours at the King's Arms, was still in progress when Strang, exhausted, collapsed upon a bench in the dining hall and the wenches brought him a jug of wine and platters of meat, fish, vegetables and salads. Nan Quick came across, smiling at him archly, and Strang remembered a surly glance or two he had received from her husband following the incident in the orchard. It was yet another problem at the back of his mind, for he felt sorry for a cuckolded husband. Besides, it could be dangerous if a husband was violent by nature as well as jealous.

Seeking to dissuade Nan from any adventure this evening, Strang wearily wiped at his forehead and said, 'Ma'am, I've had a hardish day.'

'Which, Sir Harry, followed a hardish night.' There was a touch of contempt in the manner in which she said this which irritated him. 'But it is not important, Sir Harry, and I must do my duty to my husband and attend to him.'

'I'm glad you won't lie alone, ma'am,' Strang responded.

She answered him playfully, 'Already developing the wit of a Rochester after only a day or so in town.'

'Not developing,' Strang retorted, 'it is already in the family.'

She was now amused and friendly again. 'And, Sir Harry, what a family!'

Remembering all that had happened since he arrived and the news that Nell Gwynne was his kin, all he could retort was, 'Amen to that, ma'am.'

Chapter Twelve

THE last person Strang thought of before he fell asleep and the first when he awoke, was Comfort Templegate. But on both occasions the memory of her was edged with the shadow of his many problems. The attempt on his life the night before was the largest problem of all for it seemed, on reflection, to be not the work of highwaymen. The men had used a torch which betrayed them, as they must know it would, so they could identify their victim before they struck. And their victim was to be him.

But why? It had to be Preacher Fox's work, and could be nobody else's. Why should Fox want him dead before he had discovered what Strang wished to say to him? Unless, perhaps, Strang had already been identified to Fox as one of the men who had attacked his establishment at Kensington Village and killed and wounded his followers?

Perhaps Rochester and Hawkins were right and Fox, a vicious fellow, was beyond the worth of saving, but Strang always had the frightful picture of Gordon Thomas, pilloried and broken, before him. Moreover, in balance, he could reflect, Fox had suffered more at Rochester and his hands than they at his, for all Fox had done was make off with Nell Gwynne, and his professed motives for doing this, he claimed, were noble. It was not a point that Strang felt he would argue about with anybody, for he himself thought that the stews of Drury Lane were no place for a teenage child, especially now that he had discovered Nell was either a sister or a cousin.

He felt he must persevere with the matter a little longer and must give Fox the benefit of his warning. After all, it was he and Rochester who had betrayed Fox to Redeeming Hawkins. Fox might be violently against the King, which was unforgivable, but providing he only talked – and if he could be advised to moderate his talk and be discreet – Strang thought it a job well worth the trying. He would approach Fox again, but this time he would be on his guard, and he would ensure his safety by journeying to see him only by day.

Then there were the Templegates to consider. If he could bring about a rapport between Heaven Templegate and Fox and persuade Fox to a path of moderation, he would have served the Templegates well again and be a hero in Comfort's eyes. Intolerance was the root of the problem on both the Government and Fox's sides, an aftermath of the bitterness bred in the Civil Wars, and if he could bring about a reconciliation between the warring factions, he would win the King's thanks as well. Fox had been persecuted and, because he was a man of spirit, he was striking back, bitterly and bluntly. It needed somebody like Strang, fresh from the country and not involved, to see the stupidity of it all and point the way. Strang was still abed, mulling over these thoughts, and thinking at times of Comfort Templegate, when his cousin, more drunk than he had ever seen him, arrived. He was not alone.

He was followed by a coarse, villainous looking man with a broken nose and a patch over one eye whose face was a dark brown and looked as cracked as well used leather. Behind him came one of Nan Quick's maids carrying a tray of drinks. Rochester, in sharp contrast to his companion, was handsomely attired in silk doublet and breeches of a peach colour, the material craftily ingrained with an intricate crossband motif of several colours in pattern. Rochester who could hardly stand or speak and who, by his eyes and beard, had been drinking all night, Strang judged, pulled back the drapes and showed his annoyance because Strang was sleeping alone. He claimed that Strang was insulting the family. His friend, who was heavily cloaked for the time of the year, cackled loudly at everything Rochester said, and went immediately to the fire grate. Strang sat up in bed with annoyance as he saw the man make water in the grate but, remembering he was in London, decided it was a waste of time – besides it was too late – to complain.

Rochester wouldn't let the matter be. He shook Strang's bare shoulder and said, 'Beds were made for swiving as well as sleeping. What ails you, cousin?' He saw the maid busy with the drinks, crossed to her, lifted her and would have carried her to Strang's bed. But she wriggled madly and the stranger, his work finished at the fireplace, added his cockle to the uproar as he turned.

Rochester dropped the girl heavily, ordering her away because she wasn't attractive enough, and his mood changing to one of happy laughter, he yelled, 'Cousin, we are to be rich. And you need lie with no buck-toothed heiress to gain your riches. Here,' he indicated the coarse stranger, 'is Captain Nathan Tucker, a man of many years of seafaring. He has the plan, I can raise the capital, and we will carry out a privateering expedition against those up-start Dutch.'

Captain Tucker laughed loudly and began to punch at the air about him. 'We'll war against the bastard *Butterboxes,*' he said, 'and leave them castrated and penniless on their burning ships.'

Strang slipped from the bed and began to dress. He knew that friction was growing with the Dutch because of their growing sea power which brought them into conflict with British shipping at distant trading ports, but he also knew that the King – indeed he had heard him say as much to Rochester – would be against privateering, which was only a politer name for piracy. He had to listen, however, while Rochester outlined the plan while Captain Tucker, still cackling to punctuate Rochester's words, helped himself to wine at the table.

'A pox on all *Butterboxes,*' Captain Tucker called. 'I owe them for many a scar.'

Rochester, an eloquent talker, made it sound so easy. They would slip from the Thames, sail to mid-Channel and sitting there and waiting for them – 'like virgins for swiving' – would be a Dutch transport, laden with silks from India and spices from further east. It would take but a day's work, Rochester maintained, with Tucker vigorously agreeing with him, to bring the captive up to London Port and auction both goods and ship and demand ransom for any important *Butterboxes* who might be aboard.

Eventually Strang demanded that Rochester change the subject, saying that he would discuss the matter at some later date when Rochester's critical faculties hadn't been neutralised by drink, and he then begged Captain Tucker, politely, to await them in the taproom because he had important family matters to discuss with his cousin. Captain Tucker bowed without mockery, took a decanter of wine, and left.

Rochester who was at the table helping himself to drink and using one arm to support himself, asked Strang to drink to his forthcoming success at court. 'I dine with the King at noon,' he said.

'But,' Strang protested, 'you are banned at court?'

Rochester indicated the splendour of his attire. 'Cousin, I am in love but she is as penniless as she is beautiful. She is at court this very day and I must incur the King's displeasure to see her. Besides, I must have her before the King gets her.'

'Who is she?'

But this Rochester refused to tell him yet, and Strang, abruptly changing the subject, demands to know why Rochester had kept secret from him the fact that one of their fathers was father to Nell Gwynne.

It worried Rochester for a moment that Strang had found out, but his reasons were much as Mrs Smith said they might be. Strang, who was more conscientious than he was, might feel compelled to do something about removing Nell to a good home and school which, Rochester thought, would lead to her ruin. 'She is best left in Drury Lane, cousin, where she can learn of life in the round.'

'But you saw she would flirt with me and had matters got out of hand, I might well have committed the crime of lying with my own sister!'

Rochester laughed at the thought, and then said:

'Of one thing, cousin, we can be sure. Nell's very wit and randiness points to her being a Wilmot, not a Strang. You wouldn't have been the first gallant to sleep with a cousin, which, incidentally, is an admirable way for both to learn, and should become a national pursuit, since it would do much to unite families. I must propose it as a possible parliamentary bill to the King.'

'One day,' Strang said with an edge in his voice, 'I'll beat you in discourse.'

'Discourse, never; intercourse, never.' He indicated the empty bed.

Strang quickly apologised, saying that he had been late home, and then returned to Nell Gwynne by saying that he had discovered that she had left home to stay with her uncle, a miller, at Islington Village. Rochester showed annoyance, crossed to the mantlepiece and grabbed at it for support.

'If you wish to piss, cousin, I'll thank you to go downstairs,' Strang said.

Rochester replied, 'In London fireplaces, as beds, serve for double purposes, cousin.' He turned, frowning still, and asked

Strang if he believed Mrs Smith when she said Nell was at Islington, and Strang replied that he thought she had spoken the truth. He added, 'I thought of checking by riding that way, cousin. It is little more than a mile, and the day is fine.'

Rochester looked pleased by this. 'I would be happy if you would, cousin. Though she be my sister, I have pressing matters at court. I would print a kiss on all four of my lady's cheeks before the King reaches her first.'

Strang laughed. 'Who is she cousin?'

'If I have success, Harry, you will know.'

Strang said that if he didn't know her name now he wouldn't know if Rochester had succeeded or not in truth, 'since you might substitute some other victim's name to hide your failure.'

Rochester laughed. 'At times, despite the fact you are a Strang cousin, you show a sharpness of wit.'

Pleased by this compliment, Strang found himself telling his cousin that he too was in love, and he added, 'You know her, John, or at least you have seen her. She is Mistress Comfort Templegate and, incidentally, I demand you apologise to her father.'

Strang was surprised by the look of horror that clouded his cousin's face, and he hurried to say that he was only half-joking on the matter of an apology, but it was not this which had brought the agony to his cousin's brow.

Strang wondered what could be wrong and Rochester being Rochester must need make melodrama out of the mystery for, indicating the bed, he ordered Strang to sit before he spoke. Then, striking his forehead and saying that he blamed himself for allowing Strang from his sight only a day or two after his arrival in London, he said, 'Harry, you are the world's greatest fool.'

'But why?'

'I picked quarrel with Heaven Templegate deliberately because I know him, and knowing him, I know what a dangerous man he is.'

Heaven Templegate who had been made ill by the fact that he had been forced to criticise Preacher Fox, a dangerous man? Strang found it hard to believe.

'I do not lie, cousin,' Rochester said. 'This man is a danger because he will have virile men do no more than chase the apprentice boys around Cheapside – if he has his way. He is the leader of a virulent group of Quakers, cousin, and it is his preaching that sex be banned. Not, mark you, sex only between couples who are unmarried, which would be bad enough. Good God, but sex between married couples. There are many couples – Church married – who, on becoming Shaking Quakers, as they call themselves, swear to forgo the pleasures of the marital bed.'

Strang was dumbfounded and speechless.

Rochester said, 'I see you find it hard to believe, but you are new to London, cousin. I know I jest often, but I am in deadly earnest as I speak. Yet take not my word, go ask Nan Quick or her husband or somebody else who you may trust.'

'This is absurd', said Strang, 'and for many reasons. Why, if carried through, it would mean the end of the human race.'

'That worries me less than lying alone at night,' Rochester said with a bitter chuckle.

Strang stared at the polished floorboards, then helped himself to a full mug of wine. Things began to fit to confirm what Rochester had told him. He remembered that Comfort had lost many sisters and brothers and this might have turned Heaven Templegate, in his grief, against others suffering like pain. He remembered Comfort's words that she *believed* they could be no more than friends; he remembered that it had crossed his mind, while he observed them, that some of the Shakers on the lawn appeared to be getting a sexual pleasure from their dancing, and this could, he now realised, be occasioned by long sexual abstinence.

Rochester said grimly, 'Comfort Templegate is indeed lovely, which is more the cruelty. But how can you love one so lovely if you can never lie with her? Imagine the horror of it, that one so lovely will never know the joys of love.' He added fiercely, 'Now you know why I want to skewer the old goat every time I see him in the street.'

The portent of Strang's news seemed to have both sobered and deranged Rochester, who went into a long condemnation of the religious sects which the backwash of the Civil War had left in London. He was all for shipping them off to join the rest of their kind in the Americas. He criticised the King for being tolerant about them, 'Why should he be tolerant when Templegates and Foxes are not?' he demanded. Then seeing how upset his cousin was by the news he had given him, Rochester tried to comfort him. He would soon forget Comfort Templegate, he said, when he got to court and saw how beautiful, how many, and how willing the ladies were there.

But Strang told him, 'It will be difficult to forget her, cousin, for my love for her is pure, not profane.'

Rochester sighed. He saw Strang had a problem. 'These calf things are the very hell to cure, Harry.'

Strang said, 'I think all hope has not gone. I know she is very fond of me.'

Rochester looked interested. 'Five guineas will buy a competent assassin, Harry. With Heaven gone to heaven, your influence might change the girl for the better.'

'Don't jest,' Strang said angrily.

Rochester looked surprised, for he had not been jesting. 'Then you must win her away from the old coot with your wit. It is as yet only the Greys Inn legal fraternity variety, but it will improve under my tutelage.'

Strang decided he wished to be alone, and he asked Rochester to wait in the taproom with Captain Tucker, and he would join him there. Rochester shrugged and agreed and telling his cousin not to mope, left the chamber. 'Tucker,' he said grandly from the door, 'will make all our fortunes for us, and then you can have all the beauties you want.'

Strang sat alone for long minutes nursing his sorrow. Then he decided action was the cure. First to Islington Village to look into the welfare of Nell Gwynne; and then to Shoreditch Church to have discourse with Preacher Fox.

Strang didn't go to the taproom but left a note for Rochester to say he had gone to Islington on his errand. This time he took his pistols with him in their saddle holster and Master Quick, seeing him go, called nastily, 'Good day, Sir Harry; off to the wars, are we?'

Strang didn't reply. He knew now something of the hurt which might be in the man.

Chapter Thirteen

EVEN though he was telling himself that he must forget Comfort Templegate, Strang went to Islington by way of Chancery Lane, slowing his mount as he passed the Templegate home, hoping that Comfort might see his departure. If she saw the pistols at his holsters, she might assume he was away to the country and hasten after him to give him her farewell and, perhaps, register her hope to see him soon on his return. But nobody was at the windows of the house, which was tall, of three storeys and must cost at least fifty pounds a year to rent. Strang made good time and with his arrival at the farmlands of Clerkenwell the stenches of London town were soon behind him. He breathed sweet air. Some of the farm workers looked at him with suspicion because of the heavy pistols, thinking him perhaps a gentleman of the high toby, and he was reminded what happened to highwaymen when, at Saddler's Wells, he saw a decaying body in irons hanging by the crossroads. Some urchins were having sport by dragging back the rotting corpse by a rope and letting the body fly into the road when a traveller happened by. However Strang saw their game before he reached them and was ready for them.

He saw the windmill long before he reached the village of Islington, and swung his horse towards it. A thick-set man with rosy cheeks sat by the door. He was wearing a smock covered with flour dust and smoked on a clay pipe as he watched Strang approach. It seemed to Strang that it took him a long time to reach the man while the man studied him.

Strang wished the miller good day but the miller didn't answer him and, a countryman himself, Strang recognised the type. The miller wouldn't speak until to wanted to, and that could be a great distance of time away.

Strang tried again. 'I'm looking for young Nell Gwynne,' he said.

This finally brought a response for after another long hard

look at Strang, the man said, 'What would you be wanting with her, m'lord?'

'I wish to see that she is well.'

'That you cannot see, for she isn't here.'

'Then as an interested party, my man, I would know where she is.'

The miller was silent and suddenly a woman, who had been listening, came from behind the door and, unnecessarily, demanded of the miller what the lord wanted, and when the miller told her, she confirmed the fact that Nell wasn't at Islington, and again, Strang demanded to know where he could find her. It crossed his mind that Nell had never come to Islington and that Rochester's sceptism was well founded and that Mrs Smith had put Nell, a virgin, out to bed with a gentleman for a fine fee. The thought made him angry, and Strang told the couple that he knew Nell Gwynne was their niece and that he, too, was related to her, and explained the connection. He told them his name and they recognised it, and the revelation gave spur to their tongues for they both attempted to tell him the evil tidings together and since both told slightly different versions and began at separate ends of the story, it took Strang a time to sort it out.

It seemed that Nell Gwynne had arrived safely on the post-coach the day before. But she had, a head-strong girl, been in one of her tempers, and almost immediately she had shed the best and better part of her clothing and was soon riding a horse about the pasture wearing jus her shift, with the ends flying in the breeze as she galloped.

It wasn't hard for Strang to imagine for he had a memory of Nell, wearing only a short shift, galloping down the road behind Rochester from the mansion at Kensington. The couple told him that a crowd had soon gathered, because Nell galloped well, and the woman said that she had only scolded Nell because the breeze was cool and she might catch cold, and this had brought a string of oaths and more bad temper. Nell had dismounted, gone into the mill and locked herself in the buttery; but, unfortunately, finding cider there, she was soon drunk.

When drunk, she had gone to a window overlooking the road and bawled at passersby until she soon had a crowd. 'I have many misfortunes,' she had called over and over again, 'I am a Protestant and a virgin, and I am a bastard and I am single.

If any good Quaker or Catholic can cure three of these ills, I will be content to remain a bastard.'

The old couple became vexed to the point of tears when they mentioned the religious substance in Nell's remarks, but Strang, anxious to know it all, urged them both to finish the story.

It appeared that among the crowd which had gathered, there was a young giant, who answered, 'I be Quaker and unmarried but have some experience as a fornicator and I am said to be a bit of a bastard myself. Please join me, ma'am, and come away with me.'

The crowd had roared lustily that the girl accept the offer and some, believing the miller and his wife had treated the girl badly, yelled insults at the pair, who had been forced to hurry inside the windmill and hide. They had seen enough, however, to know that the man had taken Nell away, for he had dismounted and led his horse to the door, and they had heard the brief conversation which had taken place.

The old miller looked sadly at his pipe and said, 'I don't know if there was design in it, but they knew each other. Or seemed to. For Nell said – when seeing him at the door – 'Ginger-mop! Why, I know you!'

The miller's wife said she had taken a look from the window and the man had ginger hair, and Strang was puzzled for Fox – if it was Fox – could hardly be in two places at the same time. He had seen a ginger-headed man at the Shoreditch forge, which later description from Comfort Templegate and Mrs Smith suggested was Fox. But the man at the forge said Fox was at Islington, and a man who fitted Fox's general description had, apparently, carried Nell off at about the time Strang was at Shoreditch. But Nell knew Preacher Fox and Strang could hardly imagine her leaving – willingly and happily – with him. After all, she had complained that he had treated her so badly and had shown him the marks on her buttocks to prove it.

It was a mystery, and he would only find the answer at Shoreditch. He asked the miller what road the couple had taken, and the miller said, 'Why, he looked a Quaker, said he was a Quaker, and took the direction of Hoxton and Shoreditch, and that is where many of those scoundrels live.'

'The pity of it is,' said the wife, 'that they come to Islington in great numbers to buy our cakes and bread. I warrant Nell, ruined by now, will be found in the Shoreditch parish.' She began to cry. 'Her mother will never forgive us.'

The miller attempted to comfort her. 'To bed with a Quaker is bad enough, but to offer him marriage! She is a good Protestant really, m'lord I hope neither my Lord Rochester or your good self will disown or disinherit her.'

Strang hurriedly reassured them on this point.

'Wait until she discovers the evil way these people copulate,' said the woman. 'Like animals they are, and she'll be back. Comfort yourself with that thought.'

'Rather she be a good whore, worthy of her hire like her mother,' said the miller, 'than wedded to a Quaker.' He spat viciously into the dust.

'Her mother is a whore,' said the wife, 'and she is my sister, but I take pride in the fact that she is highly rated at the trade, and nobody can ask for more from God than that they do what work he allows them to do well.'

Strang was as much concerned by the religious intolerance that the couple showed as he was by the news that Nell was again missing, and again with a man who was a Quaker and seemed to fit Fox's description. He told them to end their weeping and he would soon have Nell back to their care, and with their prayers and good wishes following him, mounted his horse and headed, at a fast clip, towards Shoreditch.

Chapter Fourteen

STRANG made several stops to rest his horse, but even so he was at Shoreditch within the hour. He pushed his horse fast, enjoying the speed, which seemed to drive all his problems away and leave him in a glow of optimism. Soon, everything would be all right, he reassured himself, and painted an idealistic picture in his mind in which Fox, subdued and sensible, had been reconciled with Heaven Templegate, in which Heaven Templegate realised the impracticalities of some of his teachings and in which – with her father's approval – Comfort put the call of the flesh before the call of God, in her father's image, and turned to Strang.

Even Nell Gwynne was saved in the moment of her ruin, discovered the virtues of patience, and went on to do great things in the theatre while Rochester, replacing the bottle for the quill, wrote fine plays in which Nell acted. At the quiet village of Hoxton, Strang got an ugly shock when he saw a supine and unconscious form locked in the village stocks. But as he trotted by the frame, he felt the glow of hope again, for the man hadn't been pulped to death by brickbats from a savage mob, but was unconscious drunk and had been placed there no doubt by the wisdom of the village elders to sleep the orgy off. The world wasn't such a bad place after all, he decided as he put the horse into a canter.

Even though he was optimistic about the outcome, Strang approached the Shoreditch Church parish with watchful care, He kept away from the main London road which led to the Bishops Gate and, instead, approached the area by taking the circuitous lanes through the village of Hoxton. He crossed the Kingsland Road at a fast clip and became lost behind the hedgerows on the northern side of the road. The ground dipped here and the hedgerows were high, but once he saw the spire of the church on his right, he would soon be about level where he judged the blacksmith's yard to be and could turn to approach it from the Hackney side.

He needed a cart track going to the right and eventually he came to one, and turned down it. Through the hedge on the left he heard the distant voices of men and judged them to be farm-workers, and then he was upon Preacher Fox and his desperate men before he realised it. There was a sudden gap in the hedge and Strang saw a meadow, a creeper-covered and dilapidated manor house and, more, a dozen or so sturdy men carrying out what appeared to be military drill. They were in line, wore similar drab Puritan clothes, and each had a broadsword sloped across his shoulder. Before them stood a thick-set man who was the ginger-headed man Strang had talked to at the nearby blacksmith's forge. Just to the right of him was another man, who looked almost like his double, was almost of the same height and had the same red hair. Strang realised the truth – they were brothers. It was easy to see which of them was Preacher Fox, however. There was an authority and a sterness and a fanaticism about the eyes and the set of one of the men's jaws which was unmistakable and, by contrast, the second brother looked amiable, lazy, and almost a jovial village idiot. The first man was the one who Strang had talked to at the forge. All this Strang saw and realised in seconds. Preacher had lied to him, possibly because he needed to think about Strang and plot a course of action, so he said that he was at Islington when, in fact, his brother was there. It was the younger, friendlier, easier brother with whom Nell Gwynne had casually, and apparently, happily left the mill of her aunt and uncle.

In that very moment as the truth dawned, Strang was seen, and a shout went up and for a deadly moment all eyes were silently upon him, and then Preacher Fox yelled a warning and sprang towards him. Strang pushed his horse forward through the gap in the hedge, waving frantically to Preacher Fox; but, at the same time, two men who had been on sentry duty along the hedge, possibly to ensure that nobody observed the military training, came into sight. Both were close, both carried pikes, and they rushed at Strang with the obvious intenion of cutting him down.

Strang heard the swishing sound their feet made in the long grass. He could see the sweat breaking on their determined and ferocious faces, and their long weapons were already aimed to spear him down. Their eyes were murderously menacing yet devoid of any personal malice, and Strang now knew how an enemy, strangers, looked on a battlefield.

Strang drew his pistols and without dismounting rested his right wrist across his left arm and aimed at the nearest man.

'Hold hard, sir, or I'll fire,' he called. But the man increased his speed to use his pike before the pistol exploded, and regretfully, feeling the first bitter acid of defeat in his mouth, Strang pulled the trigger. There wasn't time to aim for a less damaging point of the pike-man's body. He levelled on the bulk of the man, and the ball took him squarely in the trunk, and down he crashed, legs thrashing, pike skidding, and the blood bubbling up from his body.

Strang was already moving to face the second onslaught. But as he brought his second pistol up, using his left hand now for there wouldn't be time to change it to his right, the man threw the pike as he realised he didn't have the time to reach Strang before the pistol exploded. The pike was heavy, too heavy perhaps for an accurate throw, and it lost height in transit. But although it missed Strang, it caught the horse beneath him.

It was heavy. It seemed to hang in the air. It veered and drooped at the point, but it hit the horse with sufficient force to penetrate its broad chest. Strang felt the shock that convulsed the animal's body. Immediately it screeched, reared its head, and crashed to the ground. Strang fired the pistol involuntarily as he was striving to clear his legs from the stirrups, and the ball sped upwards in the air. As the animal clouted the ground, rolling to its left side, so Strang jumped clear to the right, but he skidded on the wet turf.

The pikeman was still coming, and had now paused to draw his sword, and it was all Strang could do to recover his balance and draw his own sword before the man brought his sword over with all the power he could muster in an attempt to crash through Strang's guard and decapitate him as he came up. Although he was not yet firmly on his feet, Strang managed to hold the blow. He felt the shock of it race the length of his sword arm. The man had guts but little skill and by the time he lunged against Strang again, he was ready for him. Strang lifted the blow, flicking it easily aside, sword rasped against sword, Strang flicked his wrist.

It was the oldest trick in the book but it was effective. The man parried to the left, thinking Strang would lunge from there, but Strang came in fast, sword extended, from the other side. In a flash he had placed three inches of his thirty-eight and a half-inch rapier in the sentry's groin before the man knew what was happening.

But the Fox brothers and the men who had drilled were almost on Strang, and he knew that there would be no allowance for talk, not with two of his followers down and probably dead or dying. Yet Strang could reflect bitterly that he hadn't wanted this. Why in dammation couldn't Fox talk first before resorting to violence? The man must be mad. Strang prepared to meet the inevitable end, the empty pistol in his left hand to ward off blows, the bloody sword in his right. A line of waving broadswords came at him, and Strang felt a sickness in his stomach, vomit in his throat, a turmoil of racing thoughts in his mind. The day, bright and glarish, now seemed to mock at him, and there were even birds, as if nothing was untoward, chirping merrily in the thickets. Strang felt, with a sinking gloom, that he was already dead. He deserved to die. He had been a fool. Nobody but himself was to blame.

Rochester had warned him about the fanaticism of the religious zealots, so too had Redeeming Hawkins, Heaven Templegate, even Comfort, yet with a blithe countryman's innocence Strang had charged in, thinking with his grand conceit that he could reconcile quarrels that were so deep and bitter that they called for death.

Since there was nothing else to do but try, Strang tried to reason with Preacher Fox, who was leading the advance, his face set firmly in lines of hatred and with a bright violence showing in his eyes. No, he could expect no mercy, not from men like these. He only had to look at their faces to see how naïve he had been. These, after all, were the Lord Protector's Ironsiders, the veterans of the new Model Army who had campaigned with sword and fire through England, Scotland and Ireland, committing butchery in God's name.

He managed to find his voice. 'Preacher Fox, put up your swords. I must speak with you. I bring news which puts you in some danger.'

Fox answered with a sneer. 'You have done more damage to me, Cavalier. You die first, then Rochester and then your lewd master, Charles Stuart.'

Strang had stepped back so the dead horse afforded him some small protection on his left and the ditch and the bank were directly behind him, but some ten men faced him, and all were armed, and he knew he was finished. Yet something,

something invisible and intangible, seemed to make Fox and his cohort hold back.

'You are undone, Fox,' Strang replied bitterly, 'but you do not yet know it. Your plot and your plans are known.'

Fox held back for a reason, and Strang did not know it. Nor would he. There had been a third pikeman on patrol, but in the road beyond the hedge, and it was he who came silently up behind Strang and, while on the opposite side of the ditch, brought the end of his pike down with a ferocious blow across Strang's head. For a moment Strang rocked and teetered. Flaming stars criss-crossed his vision and his brain seemed to explode, and then he was falling into a deepening pit of darkness.

Chapter Fifteen

It was a dripping sound he heard first – loud, hollow, persistent, carefully timed, and in his sorry condition and his uncomfortable position, he knew it to be the lap, lap of his own blood draining from him. It was dark, but not so completely dark as death, so he knew he was still alive – if barely so. In his half-conscious state, he assumed he was in a dungeon run by the State and Redeeming Hawkins was officiating functionary. Yes, he could see the evil rascal now, smirking in a little void before him, and repeating what he had already told Strang once that he was too trusting of his fellow man. Certainly he had been too trusting of Master Fox, but was that any reason for Hawkins to rack him? For certainly he was being racked, with his hands fastened high above him. He had done nothing wrong, but then Redeeming Hawkins would remind him that all men are guilty, and if he couldn't rack you for something you had done, rest assured, he would rack you for something you had left undone. He hadn't told Hawkins what he knew about Fox and Shoreditch, and certainly that was a rackable offence.

From far off, Strang could hear footsteps. They were hollow and measured like the dripping sounds – and they held another kind of menace and terror. It would be the executioner coming. Strang raised his voice to protest. He didn't care what the offence was, he would refuse to be hanged at Tyburn. He was a baronet, not a knight, and Redeeming Hawkins must get protocol right, and as a nobleman he must die by the axe at the Tower.

On came the footsteps, and Hawkins nodded, entirely in agreement. Put not your trust in princes, Strang heard himself saying. But Fox had been no prince. The Earl of Strafford had said that twenty years since as he had hobbled to the scaffold, betrayed by the present King's father. Charles II had betrayed a great man, too, Montrose in Scotland, though it couldn't be helped. Still, he, Harry Strang, was in London to serve the King – if Master Preacher Fox would let him.

Drip, drip and slap, slap, as the feet approached. He was almost dead so what point was there in digesting a lesson about trust? He was Fox's prisoner. He realised that as his head began to clear. It all came back to him. A sharp reminder of the blow from which his head throbbed with the memory of it; his horse, the finest on the estate, dead; two of Fox's men dead or dying. He must be in the old house, creeper-covered, Tudor in style, which he remembered noting had been built on the cheap since there was a lack of windows, for it had been constructed when only millionaires could afford glass. A Tudor hunting lodge, he had thought, when first seeing it, built more than a hundred years before, when there was still wild game this close to London. Possibly Henry VII had used it, for his son, wicked Henry VIII, had been forced to hunt further afield at Putney and Richmond. The house was alive with sounds, and sounds apart from the persistent drip of what he thought had been his blood and those oncoming feet. There were many men in the rooms above him making the floorboards creak and the muffled sounds of their voices strangely distant and hollow. But Nell was here somewhere. Nell Gwynne! He presumed she had left Islington with Preacher's brother. But he hesitated. Although she was the only one who might save him, it was but a slender hope. She was but a girl. Moreover she was possibly a partial prisoner too, even if she had arrived voluntarily.

Arrived voluntarily! She had come to be with the more cheerful of the Fox brothers. She might have been ruined by him now, which she was anxious should happen, and if this were so she would have no time or sympathy for Strang now, or very little. She would be a hundred per cent for the man who had bedded her and his enemies would become her enemies. Nell was kind, might like him even, but he could see little or no hope in that direction. The best she could do for him would be to plead for a painless end.

If he got the opportunity, if he saw Nell alone – which was unlikely – then he could appeal to the sweetness in her nature, and attempt to persuade her to help him, but only God knew how and to do what. He remembered something else and it made him sit up and the movement made his head ache again. If Nell had been so smitten by the Fox brother that she couldn't take the trouble to help him, why he could play his ace card!

Nell was either his sister or his cousin, and if he made her aware of this fact, she simply couldn't let him die without making some attempt to help him.

Better sister than cousin, he decided, for there would be danger for her. Rochester favoured the theory that he was sister to Nell because of her quick-wit and humour and Rochester could be right, but he now sought for possible evidence he could present to her to show that in fact he was her brother and that she was a Strang, not a Wilmot. He must think it out quickly for his very life might depend upon him showing the girl that they were brother and sister.

The Strangs were the duller side of the family, and the Wilmots were the brighter and the most sensual, but even if this pointed to Nell being a Wilmot, Strang had to admit – and Nell must agree – that physically she favoured Strang more than Wilmot. Thinking feverishly along these lines, thinking of bone structure, shapes of noses, hair colouring, and suchlike, Strang suddenly paused. He felt a deepening shame. How could he become so much the craven coward that he could invent such a tale at this time to hide behind a girl's short shift? God, so close to death, and he couldn't face it squarely and bravely! He was a Strang, and in antiquity Strangs had been captains, knights, sailors, soldiers and adventurers.

Quickly, angrily, Strang dismissed the matter and then put his mind to his surroundings and those footsteps he continued to hear. Were they coming nearer, or did he just imagine it?

It took a time for Strang to discover that the footsteps were definitely coming nearer. They seemed to have started, oddly, somewhere high in the wall, and the increasing sound of their nearness somehow indicated that they were descending stairs. A door creaked open somewhere and almost immediately there was a pale glow of candle light. Strang attempted to see all things at once, the wall to which he was fastened with his hands above his head, the cellar-like surroudings and the many goods it contained. He recognised that he was in some sort of armoury by the shapes of the things he saw – barrels, boxes, muskets and swords, pistols and daggers and horse equipment neatly stacked or racked against the walls. Behind the advancing candle, which was on some sort of tray, there was a vague, slight figure, who then spoke, and he recognised Nell Gwynne's voice. Elation and excitement made him respond immediately, 'Here, Nell, sweet sister,' he called, adding *sister* before he realised it and could stop it.

'Shhrrr, not so loud,' she whispered. She indicated the other direction to the one she had entered, 'There are guards beyond a door there.'

Her arrival and the implication of her remarks that she was on his side, which meant there was now hope, overwhelmed Strang with an excitement he couldn't contain, and so many questions sprang to his mind which demanded answers. She had folded down beside him, the candle held close, the better to see him and judge the damage to him. She told him that only Robin Fox knew she was here and that she had come to him down the back staircase from the servants quarters and the door there was not locked because nobody seemed to be aware of an entrance there. But there were no windows to the back of the house, she added, and no door leading to the grounds there. 'I'm glad to find you somewhat recovered,' she whispered; 'I feared, by that clout you received, you might be dead.'

This said, she then turned to discussing Robin Fox, and how she had persuaded him to let her come and see him and bring him food and drink. She talked about Robin Fox with an affection which dismayed Strang but added, which again made him feel hopeful, that he was easy to handle and was weak in her capable hands.

'There is hope then?' Strang demanded.

Nell was doubtful on this point, but reluctant to admit it and depress Strang again. She said, 'There are problems. Robin is easy but yields more to Preacher than he does to me. Hence, against Robin's wishes, I am still unruined.' She shifted slightly, lowered the candle to her thighs, and lifted her short skirt. 'Look, that damned Preacher beat me again, and Robin let him. And all because I said fornication was a good thing when he forbade Robin to bed me until he had wed me.'

Strang bent forward but couldn't see the marks of the thrashing in the poor light, but he hurried to declare, 'Nell, a man who won't defend you, especially from a beating, is worth nothing. Robin, I firmly declare, is not for you. And since your mother has acquainted me with the fact that we are closely related, that you are my sister in fact, I must do my duty, I fear, and say that you must wait a worthier candidate as lover and husband.'

Nell snorted derisively, 'If I am sister to anybody, it is to Rochester, and only cousin to you, but it is a story I refuse to believe, and only put to me by Rochester because he does not fancy me but tells me that instead to spare my feelings.' She laughed again. 'At most you are my cousin, Sir Harry, and are not forbidden to bed with me.'

Strang was pleased by her reply. Before he could bed with her, he must be got out of here, and the implication of what she said suggested she had a plan. 'You are still family, cousin,' he said softly, 'so I feel compelled to extend to you my care and protection.'

'But, sir,' she said brightly, 'it is you who are fastened to the wall and now wait my care and protection.'

Strang felt helpless and ashamed. It angered him, and he said, 'Nell, this is no time to play the fool. Please release me. We are in grave danger.'

'I will free you,' she said softly, 'but don't try and blackmail me by calling me family or putting the heavy hand of parental authority upon me. I'm sick to death of all that.'

'That,' snapped Strang, 'is because you have been allowed to run wild in the gutters of Drury Lane for so long.'

'Your boorish manner, Sir Harry, only confirms to me that I'm more a Wilmot than a Strang and makes me delay in assisting you. As you say this is a deathly matter.'

'I'm sorry,' said Strang, 'but I would have you treat this matter both as deadly and change my circumstances for the better with all speed.'

'Right,' she said, 'but first a promise. You and I have a chamber appointment on my fifteenth birthday.'

Strang found his temper rising again. He was trussed and waiting certain death, but Nell dallied and played the flirtatious bawd with him. God, had the entire world gone mad and lost its judgement? Any moment, from fear or jealousy, Robin Fox might arrive to see what delayed Nell, for she said he was overawed by his more powerful and fanatical brother. But he contained his anger. This was no time to pick a quarrel with the strong-willed Nell. 'You have a knife, do cut me free. While you do that, tell me what you know of this house and its occupants. And I insist, Robin Fox or no, that you leave immediately with me, lest they blame my escape on you.'

She agreed, but demanded that he first agree to the appointment for her birthday, and this he did, and she began to saw vigorously at the ropes which bound his wrists to the ring in the wall above his head. To get close, she had to place a leg on either side of him – and deliberately or not, he didn't know and couldn't argue – she pressed her body against his head, and he felt the rub of her smooth thighs against his cheeks and was almost suffocated by the material of her dress.

It crossed his mind that he should protest, but he went against this idea for she might argue and it would mean more time wasted, and she would have a point if she claimed that this was no time for convention and niceties. This led to the question of whether there was something wrong with him – a touch of the Puritan disease caught at the Templegate home – that made him ponder such a light and incidental matter as Nell's nether limbs being in such a proximity to his face. Damn it, life was more important. He managed at times to get his breath and when she went down in her up and down sawing motion, he managed to roll the odd question or two from his tongue, and she talked about the house as she worked. But it was a poor knife and a stout rope held him, and it all took valuable time. If later he was to be suspicious, and think perhaps Nell had been longer than needed at the rope and that it was not necessary for her to be so close, for the ring was not that high, well, since he owed her his life, it would be churlish to mention such a minor matter.

While she hacked at the rope, Nell told him that Preacher Fox and his men, all Ironsiders and extremist former members of the Fighting Quakers and the Fifth Monarchy Men, were now banded together in an organisation called the Sword of Vengeance. They wanted revenge on the King and his Government for the despoilation of the remains of Oliver Cromwell, which had been brought from his grave and hanged at Tyburn. Robin talked freely about his brother's plans, Nell said, and though he was only a corporal now, Robin was envisaging the day when he would be a general in the Second New Model Army. Strang knew now that Preacher Fox was intending to do more than talk against the King and was already condemned, along with his followers.

'What do they plan for me?' he demanded.

She hesitated, but Strang pressed her again, and she said, 'He wishes that all his men be bloodied and have a hand in your finish so that none can accuse the other. You will be shot down by musketry at dawn in the garden.'

Strang swallowed painfully and his throat went dry. 'What is the time now?'

'It is evening still.'

Strang felt his hands free. Nell, sensibly, had left the binding about his wrists so that he could hold his hands against the ring should guards come. At least he was loose and around him there were guns and swords. If he were to die it would not be as a helpless animal.

Nell explained the geography of the old hunting lodge. The cellar door was at the front of the house, but this was locked. Even if he got out this way, there would be guards to contend with in the hall by the front door. She had come down by the servants staircase which came from the top floor to the cellar but there were no doors leading from this to the other floors. There was no backdoor either, she told him again, and the only way out was by climbing to the top storey – the small rooms where the servants had been quartered – and coming back down by the main staircase.

Strang remembered the dripping water – if water it was – and thought there must be some airing grating leading to the garden. First however, Nell must return to Robin Fox. She had been away too long. He told her to rejoin him as soon as possible after the household had gone to sleep and wanted to know if they locked her in for the night.

'They don't,' she replied, 'but I sleep in a room with Robin. We have separate beds, for Preacher demanded it, but we are permitted to bundle for a time, fully clothed and with a board between us on the same cot, for kisses and touches.'

'Then carry through this routine,' said Strang, 'and come as soon as you can.'

'It takes Robin a time to fall asleep because he becomes so aroused at the bundling. Kissing and touching, he claims, leaves him bitterly frustrated.'

'Do what you can, Nell,' Strang said quickly, 'to put him into a sleep.'

'What do you suggest?' she demanded, playfully.

But Strang, in no mood for humour and reluctant to suggest that she submit to ruin, said testily, 'Nature will show you a swift way, ma'am.'

She laughed at his disgruntlement and said, 'I will go a little further than before.'

'But not too far, kinsman,' Strang said swiftly.

'Further but not far,' she agreed, and she bent suddenly, kissed him, and turned away. 'Eat your supper, Sir Harry, for it will give you strength for what will follow.'

'I thank you for it, Nell, and all you have done so far.'

'You have an extra interest in the meat,' she called, as she left, and laughingly added, 'it is from your horse.'

Strang shrugged with regret but began to eat.

Chapter Sixteen

AFTER Nell had gone, Strang inspected the damage caused to his head by the blow from the pike. He discovered, when he got to his feet, that his body ached in every part. His clothes were ripped but he could look upon that with a sort of Rochester-like calm. After all, he hadn't yet paid for them. And, unless Nell helped to free him, he never would. He was surprised to find that fear was furthest from his thoughts. It was as if he was already away from the house. The fact that his hands were free and that he was surrounded by weapons made the difference. Nell said they would kill him in the morning and that was several hours away yet. His head was most tender to the touch. There was a bump the size of a duck's head on his head and there was grit in his hair – either dried mud or blood. He reached for the jug Nell had left him, and drank thirstily from it. It was milk and water mixed, it was ice cold, and he felt much better afterwards – almost optimistic.

Next, holding the candle before him, he explored the cellar. It was packed with the material of war. He selected two brace of heavy pistols, loaded them with powder and ball, and deposited them close to the ring in the wall. He found a sword with a balance he liked, and placed this, hidden, near at hand.

The dripping sound was still with him, and he decided to investigate its whereabouts. He traced it by its sound. There was a narrow airing grate giving on to the garden, the cavity choked with grass, and Strang, hopefully, cleared away the deposit of a century, but there was no escape here. The grille was only three feet wide and about six inches high, and iron pegs at intervals narrowed the gap.

There was a rain barrel to the right of the grille which was over-spilling, forming a puddle, which again over-spilled and caused water to drip into the cellar. To the left of the grate, the grass was dry and Strang loaded another brace of pistols and placed them, with another sword, on the grass outside as a plan began to evolve in his mind. He then sat down to eat some of the food and when he had consumed all he wanted, he placed the tray behind the barrels.

It was some time later when Strang heard footsteps to the far right, in the opposite direction from where Nell had arrived, and he waited until he heard a key grate in a lock before he put out the candle, hid it, then seated himself on the ground and placed his hands on the ring above him.

A moment later the light of a lantern flickered across the barrels.

Then the men were all about him and the lamp was held high and Strang, pretending semi-cousciousness, and with his eyes pretending to blink in the sudden light, heard Fox's voice demanding to know if he was awake. He felt a spasm of relief. If Fox needed to know whether he was conscious, betrayal from Robin or Nell hadn't brought him here. Rough hands gripped Strang's face and the lantern was lowered, and somebody said, 'He's conscious, Colonel.'

'Then give him water,' said Fox.

Water slopped around Strang's mouth and face. It was so cold and in such quantities that it made him startle and gag and it was all he could do to keep his hands hard against the ring. Then a man wiped the water from his mouth with his hands, and stood back. Strang saw Fox before him, an imposing figure as ever, demanding both respect and obedience with his stance. A copy of the Lord Protector, Strang thought, but without the warts.

Fox said pleasantly, 'You seem much improved, Harry Strang. Yes, I do know you, though your business puzzles me. You forced me to lie to you and then ambush you, and still you return. This is important business indeed.'

'I am friendly with Master Heaven Templegate,' Strang began, but Fox snorted at mention of the name. 'That fool. He would cure the country's ills by reducing the birthrate to nil. But, Master Strang, pray continue.'

'Sir Harry, Colonel, if you don't mind. I question not your right to call yourself a colonel. Do me the like courtesy of addressing me by my title, or address me not at all.'

'I will address any man by a title, sir, which he has earned by ability and merit. But please continue.'

'I don't profess to agree with Heaven Templegate in every regard,' said Strang; 'but his sincerity is beyond question. He seemed most upset by the fact that you have taken a different and more violent path to his own. It was my hope that I might bring a reconciliation between the various Quaker factions and a lessening of violence.'

Strang had no intention now of giving Fox the original reason why he wished to meet him. He now knew he was wrong and Redeeming Hawkins and Rochester had been right. Fox was out to make more than verbal protest against the King and his Government; and Strang had no intention of telling him that Redeeming Hawkins had been informed about him.

Fox considered this. There was a long pause. Strang looked up at the four men who faced him in the pale yellow light and hoped none of them would think to check his bindings. His loaded pistols and the sword were safely out of sight and it would take a better light than the lantern for them to be seen. The story sounded implausible to Strang's ears, but he saw no derision on the faces of the men.

Finally Fox said, 'You are a country fool, sir, a simpleton, naïve. I didn't think there could be many left – not even in remote country districts. You ar new to London, I hear. It is a pity you must die for your intentions, if useless, are guided by kindness.'

'Why must I die?' Strang snapped.

'Because you have seen too much and because you have killed my comrades. But, sir, one more question. When you arrived today, you made mention of a plot. But who told you I was plotting?'

'I am not so much of a fool, sir, that I cannot deny what my eyes show me. First I saw you making swords, then I saw you drilling soldiers, and striving to keep both matters secret. I must assume that you are not with General Monck's forces and hold the King's Commission.'

'Monck is a despicable traitor and turncoat, Master Strang, and will pay for it on the gallows, never fear.'

'Monck, colonel, is a democrat. He believes the Army must be servant of the Government not the Government servant of the army.'

'I refuse to debate politics with a prisoner and a cavalier,' said Fox. 'I never held the King's commission, nor ever will, but I held the Lord Protector's, and through many a campaign. It seems that once more we must be forced to take the field and show by our better soldiering that God is on our side.'

'The sooner you are taken and hanged, sir, the better for all,' said Strang.

Fox ignored the remark. He had one more point he wished answered.

'Do you know a child named Nell Gwynne?'

'I do. She is a protége of my kinsman, the Earl of Rochester.'

'We can guess what use he has for her when she ripens. But you attended with John Wilmot in an attack on my residence at Kensington. And now you visit me here while Nell Gwynne is here.'

Strang managed to convey a contempt for Rochester and the girl in his reply. 'I did accompany my kinsmen on some madcap escapade, colonel. I know not the ins and outs of the matter. And I am surprised to hear that the urchin is here.' Strang saw no reason why Fox should not believe this since he had shown an interest in Fox's activities at Shoreditch before Nell Gwynne had arrived here.

Fox seemed to be satisfied. Now he showed an impatience to be gone. 'Your problems, sir, are almost ended. It is a pity you didn't remain in the remoteness of the country and pried into village matters as a country squire. It would suit your intellect the better.'

'Why must I die?' Strang protested. 'Please allow me the right to sue and plead for my life.'

Fox paused. 'There are several reasons why you have forfeited your life, sir. But perhaps the best is that Master Tom Sainsbury, one of my men, and a man of great ability, died not an hour past from the wound you gave him.'

Strang snapped, 'It was kill or be killed. I would remind you, sir, that I was outnumbered and your men attacked first, without waiting for me to speak.'

Fox gestured the matter aside, 'In times of turmoil, sir, justice needs to take a back pew. I'm sure God will find justice for you and allow you a place in Heaven.'

There was no sarcasm in Fox's voice, but the sheen of violence Strang had noticed earlier showed in his eyes even in this poor light. Strang felt he needed to protest still further against his execution unless Fox suspected something. He said, 'I was wronged. Would one man, even if a hated cavalier, attack so many? The attack came from your men on your order, sir.'

'I have seen a cavalier attack an army, Master Strang,' said Fox. 'I do not deny a cavalier his courage and I hope you will now show some. I saw your Charles Stuart – the man you call King – in action at Worcester. He attempted to rally those foreign troops, those laggardly Scots, and attack our positions even though we out-numbered him more than twice over. Be as brave as your King, sir, and die, at least, with my respect.'

'I will die bravely, colonel, but for my self respect, not for yours.'

'Well said, Master Strang. Fox had turned. 'Leave him light and give him water every two hours of the clock,' he said. And then he was gone, and the door was locked, and Strang was alone with the lamp on the barrel. Time dragged. Two hours seemed like four and Strang was back at the ring when a trooper, a country boy, gruff but not unkind, brought him a ladle of water. Another long wait after his departure and noises in the house above him had long since stilled, and Strang guessed it was the middle of the night, and yet Nell Gwynne had not returned.

Several times he went to the small door at the rear of the house through which the girl had entered the cellar, listened, and heard no sounds. But in the meantime he made his plans and carried out his arrangements – and these must be plans he would keep secret from the girl when she arrived. Fox must be stopped and even assuming he got safely free, there wouldn't be time to get to Whitehall, warn General Monck, and for him to return to Shoreditch with his regiment of Coldstream Guards before Fox would know that he had escaped and would raise the alarm. It was up to Strang to deal with these deadly enemies of the King in what way he could. Again the guard called to give him water and Strang asked the man the time and was shocked to discover that it was three o'clock. Nell had forsaken him. Either that or Robin Fox refused to sleep or Nell herself had fallen asleep. God, he must forget about her and find his own route to freedom. He was at the small door – locked on the opposite side – and wondering if the noise of him hacking through it with an axe would betray him, when he heard light footsteps on the stairs through the door. Pistol in hand, he listened and waited.

It was Nell. 'Here is a virgin, sir, who is ready,' she called sweetly through the woodwork. . . .

Chapter Seventeen

HER levity astonished Strang, and it made him angry because it made him, simultaneously, aware of his own fear which, because of the activity he had given himself while he waited, had been partially hidden. But Nell showed no fear. Nothing about her behaviour suggested she was aware of the fact that they both hazarded their lives. Yet, since she had told him he was to die at dawn, she was aware of the desperate situation. By aiding him, she was risking her own life.

He was yet to discover what an amazing Pandora's box of tricks Nell Gwynne was. Other people needed alcohol to make them fizzle, but Nell had some inner strength that radiated its own form of intoxication, and it functioned at the most inopportune moments. It would eventually attract the love of King Charles, but at the moment it vexed Strang sorely.

She giggled as she came through the door, naughtily saying she felt like a kitchen wench must feel when going to her master's bedroom in the dead of night.

Strang saw no connection and he snapped, 'What kept you?'

She blamed Robin Fox who had been in a great fever of agitation, she said, because he had promised his brother he wouldn't swive with her until they were married. 'And Preacher won't allow us to marry,' she said, 'until all my sins have been well and truly prayed away. I need do much more praying before Robin can do any swiving and the thought of the delay upsets him. But there, he sleeps now, and only after I was forced to take him roughly in hand.'

She would have continued in a like vein, but Strang ordered her to come to her senses and face up to the danger they were in. 'First temper from one, and now from the other,' she complained. 'But never fear, cousin, I have planned well.'

She told him how they would get from the house and Strang liked it and relaxed. He didn't tell her that he had a plan of his own which he would put into execution as soon as they reached the garden, for he did not know how fond she was of Robin Fox.

They went up the narrow staircase with Nell leading the way. The wooden slats creaked abominably, but the old house was a hive of muffled sounds. There was little space and the staircase was rounded as in a tower and Strang was bent throughout the journey and reminded of the many bruises on his body. When they got to the door on the top storey, Nell signalled him that nobody was about by wiggling her bottom at him when she could, just as easily, have waved him forward with her hand. Because of the age of the building and the diseased state of the woodwork, they had no hope of getting down the main staircase without making noise; but Nell had a plan for this.

She walked down openly, boldly and noisily, and the movements she made disguised those of Strang's, who followed behind her. When they reached the last flight, Strang bent. There was lantern light below and a man stood by the door, and he watched Nell as she came to the bottom.

'Why are you up, Mistress Nell?' demanded the guard. His voice, though friendly, suggested that she was doing wrong.

Strang recognised the voice. It was the country yokel who had brought him water. Nell brightly answered him that the horsemeat, possibly because it was a royalist's mount, had soured her stomach, and she wished to go to the woods on private business.

'But there is a pail in the privy upstairs?'

'So well-used, sir, that it would make me sicker.'

The man laughed. 'But I can't let you loose without a guard, Nell.'

'Then accompany me – providing you wait at a distance and attempt no gallantries.'

'I wouldn't be familiar, ma'am,' the youth said in a shocked voice.

'You are kind. Kinder than Preacher. Look you at what he did to my poor bottom.'

Strang shuddered and swore from his place of hiding. Nell had done enough to get them free, but now she had to over do it and delay to show the boy her beaten buttocks. She was a damned exhibitionist. He peered above the balustrade and saw them standing by the door, Nell with her shift lifted.

The guard was confused and on the point of panic, and Strang was forced to appreciate the method in Nell's madness.

The guard was sympathetic, but at the same time he strived to explain that Colonel Fox was not really an unjust man, and also forbid Nell to show him what was really only for Robin Fox's eyes, and then after they had been married.

'All I said to earn the beating,' said Nell, 'was that I had met King Charles and found him so attractive that I'd like to fuck with him.'

'Good God, Nell, you didn't,' said the guard, now shocked.

'Perhaps I did wrong, but it was a word I heard often in the gutter and Preacher shouldn't have beaten me for it. Though I do appreciate why, since the Preacher likes neither the King nor fucking.'

'Please!' the young man implored. 'Go quick about your business, and return upstairs.'

'Oh, I am sorry, but it just slipped out – as King Charles said to the Countess of Castlemaine.'

'I will pray for you, Nell,' said the guard. 'You are not bad, but you have been around those evil places, the theatres, too long. They be the devil's people doing the devil's work.'

'You can say that twice,' said Nell. 'In the meantime my stomach tells me I have work to do.'

Poised on a step that would creak at any moment, perspiring freely, Strang felt relief that Nell had ended the conversation. It seemed, to him, that she might next launch into the story of her life.

Strang waited only until they had stepped through the porch into the garden. There was a huge key inside the door and it made a fearful rasping sound as he freed it from its rusted lock. He took the key, stepped onto the porch, pulled the front door shut, and turned the key in the lock. Either he had made enough sound for the sentry to hear him or he had looked round and perceived that the front door had closed, for there came a shout and footsteps.

Strang saw him in the light of the moon, advancing openly, and suspecting nothing untoward. He couldn't see Strang, waiting with his pistol ready, for he was crouched against the blackness of the wall and door. Strang felt a momentary regret. He didn't want to kill this simple lad. He was decent enough, and knew nothing of the world and politics, but had the misfortune to be reared in a village or a family which had fallen under the spell of Preacher Fox's eloquence. He could, quite have easily, have been reared in a village where cavalier sentiments had sway. That was the tragedy of it, but it wouldn't ligthen the blow that Strang intended to strike.

The guard reached the porch and stepped forward to shove the door, and Strang, summoning all the power he could muster, hit the man with the butt of his pistol on the nape of his neck. There was a quick painful yelp, and then the man crashed to the ground. Strang dragged him away from the door and jettisoned the key into the bushes. Nell came running to join him. For once her voice was anxious. 'You haven't killed the lad?' she demanded.

Strang had hit him harder than he intended because of his own desperation and fear, and thought perhaps the guard had gone. But he reassured Nell by saying, with confidence and conviction, that the lad was only put to sleep.

'Why do you bring him? Why not leave him there?' she demanded. Strang dare not tell her the drastic plan he had in mind. 'Go wait by the trees,' he said impatiently, 'I will join you in a minute.' He decided to save time and give Nell a chore to keep her busy. He dropped the guard's legs and said, 'Take him with you, to the trees, and well away from the house.'

'Why?'

Strang didn't dare tell her. He had found a Catholic remedy for a Quaker ill. Guy Fawkes had said it not yet fifty years before – 'Drastic diseases call for drastic remedies.' It had given Strang the idea. The thing to do was to keep Nell busy so that she couldn't interfere. He ordered her to take the guard's legs and drag him to the trees beyond the garden and wait for him there.

He hurried away, saying that he would be back within a minute or so. Strang ran around the side of the house until he reached the water barrel which served as his landmark.

He parted the tall grass and saw the pale light of the lamp on the ledge just inside the grille and the bundle of kindling he had placed beside it. In a moment he had lit the kindling from the lamp and tossed it through the grate onto combustibles he had heaped beneath the window. Shortly the cellar began to glow and he knew the rubbish was well alight. He was surprised to find that he was bathed in sweat and breathing heavily yet had not carried out any actions that were unduly energetic. It was the action that he was carrying out, which would take so many lives, that ruffled him.

With the fire reflecting brightly, Strang hurried around the back of the house, instead of going straight back to the front, for he wanted to check that Nell had been right when she said there were no windows or doors at the back of the house. There was little to see, however, because the trees and the brush had been permitted to grow close to the wall, but that suggested the builder had saved the enormous expense of buying glass by having a plain wall there, for you would hardly let trees block out windows.

Nell Gwynne startled on his return. Dragging the guard and a sudden attack of nerves had made her sweat too, and she demanded to know what manner of mischief he was set upon. 'I believe I know where the horses are stabled,' she said, 'and if you come now, we will find them.'

'Soon,' he snapped, 'but now we lie low and wait.'

'But why?'

He took her firmly by the arm and forced her down in the grass beside him. The tension in his manner reached her but she did not try to free herself and for once her jesting was stilled.

The house was black and quiet in the moonlight and it remained so for perhaps a minute more, with Strang worrying that his fire had aborted, and then a vivid blue flash, blinding in its very intensity, illuminated the garden, and was followed a second later by a roar of thunder more loud than any thunder Strang had ever witnessed. The very ground beneath them trembled and seemed to split, and bright shafts of flame, burst from every opening in the house, to be followed by spurts of burning fire from every window and door which had been blown by the explosion. The old house seemed to have bulged outward and upward like some huge animal mortally struck, and then began to sink to its end in a pit of flame. Although they were at a distance, the hot blast of the explosion reached them and scorched their hands and faces, and soon pieces of burning wreckage crashed on the garden and among the trees about them.

Nell Gwynne spoke to him and even though he looked at her grim and tortured features, Strang could only guess at what she said. Her Robin was in that mass of burning and twisted furniture and floorboards and must already be dead – his accursed brother with him.

The guard still lay unconscious, perhaps even dead, and Strang knew it was time to go. His throat was dry, his head ached, his ears buzzed and itched from the effects of the explosion, and he felt at any moment that he would be sick. He wanted to go, and yet he wanted to stay and watch to the very end, the fearful holocaust he had caused. His eyes were drawn to the burning inferno as if magnitised.

It was as though a pagan ancestor reminded him of some pagan rite, and a devil's lust worked inside him. He could visualise the flames wrecking the interior, where the rotten beams had already been turned to powder by the explosives, and where everything, and everybody, was being sucked down to the flames which belched from the cellar below. What made it the more horrific for Strang was the knowledge that had Nell not come finally to release him, he would have ignited the powder in the cellar while he remained inside, determined, if he had to die, to take Fox and his desperadoes with him.

Now Nell Gwynne, tearful and violent, brought him back to the present. She had recovered and her shock and horror had been replaced by anger. She punched at him with her free hand as she tried to break his grip on her with the other, spitting oaths and curses at him, calling him a brute and a murderer.

Strang did not strike back, but eventually caught hold of her flaying fist and gripping her by both hands, pulled her through the trees and away from the house that now burnt fiercely and brightly behind them. He left the guard who, if still alive, was at a safe distance.

She didn't fight any longer to free herself from his grasp but was content, while she followed him, to continue to curse him, but now in a softer, almost trance-like manner. Eventually, he would counsel her and assure her that it was the only way, for desperate diseases do, unfortunately, call for desperate remedies. She wouldn't see that now, not while she was in sight of the burning house with Robin's cooking flesh near her nostrils. But tomorrow she would see the sense of it.

Strang reached the lane and hurried his pace, holding Nell by one hand, and she came behind him. The flames were bright still, lighting the countryside, and he was anxious to be lost in the narrow, hedge-lined lanes of Shoreditch and Hoxton before the cottagers came hurrying to see the fire. By the time they crossed the Kingsland Road and reached the village of Hoxton, Nell had ceased cursing him and was crying softly. Strang continued to hold her hand. People were at their doors and in the roads looking towards the blaze, but Strang took care and they were not seen.

It was some two miles of walking before they reached London town near Holborn, and throughout the journey – during which Nell did not speak once – Strang had to take care to avoid people brought out to watch the flames in the distance after being awoken by the explosion. When they got to Clerkenwell it didn't matter, for nobody could know they had come from Shoreditch.

Strang the country boy, and with scarcely a week of living in town, felt better when London was close at hand. There was something comfortable about London, and he was fitting into it like a cloak. The very voice of the Watch, calling the hour, as they neared Drury Lane, gave him assurance, for there was good humour in the man's peppery manner. 'Six of the clock on a fine morning, with a house burning brightly to the north-east. Otherwise all is well, and now's the time, if any of you be awake, to turn to her and do it again.'

Strang laughed and the Watch laughed and waved as, still holding Nell by the hand, Strang continued on his way. Daylight was bright behind the housetops of Drury Lane, and no doubt finding all the doxies innocently asleep in their beds, when Strang led Nell to her mother's house in Old Bone Yard. There was a firmness in his step and there would be a confidence, like Rochester had, in his manner, for while he could yet feel pity for those he had been forced to kill, the act of killing them had proved to him that he was a man.